THE CALLER

M. A. COMLEY

And

TARA LYONS

Published by Jeamel Publishing limited
Copyright © 2016 M A Comley and Tara Lyons
Digital Edition, License Notes
This ebook is licensed for your personal enjoyment only. This ebook may not be re-sold or given away to other people. If you would like to share this book with another person, please purchase an additional copy for each recipient. If you're reading this book and did not purchase it, or it was not purchased for your use only, then please return to the site and purchase your own copy. Thank you for respecting the hard work of these authors.

This is a work of fiction. Names, characters, places and incidents are a product of the author's imagination or are used fictitiously, and any resemblance to actual persons living or dead, business establishments, events or locales is entirely coincidental.

ISBN-13: 978-1533589132

ISBN-10: 1533589135

This book is dedicated to our families for putting up with our exceedingly long hours.

Thank you to the wonderful friends and fans who have supported our new venture and for the never-ending support of all The Book Club members whose daily antics keep us sane.

Special thanks as always go to our talented editor Stefanie Spangler Buswell and to Karri Klawiter for her cover design expertise.

Huge thanks go to our wonderful proofreader, Joseph Calleja, for spotting all the lingering nits.

OTHER BOOKS BY
TARA LYONS
In the Shadows
Web of Deceit (DI Sally Parker Novella with M A Comley)

Keep in touch with the author at
www.facebook.com/Taralyonsauthor
www.taralyonsauthor.blogspot.co.uk
Twitter: @Taralyonsauthor
Instagram: Taralyonsauthor

OTHER BOOKS BY
M A COMLEY
Blind Justice
Cruel Justice
Impeding Justice
Final Justice
Foul Justice
Guaranteed Justice
Ultimate Justice
Virtual Justice
Hostile Justice
Tortured Justice
Rough Justice
Dubious Justice
Calculated Justice
Twisted Justice
Forever Watching You (DI Miranda Carr thriller)
Wrong Place (DI Sally Parker thriller)
No Hiding Place (DI Sally Parker thriller)

Web of Deceit (DI Sally Parker Novella with Tara Lyons)
Evil In Disguise – a novel based on True events
Deadly Act (Hero series novella)
Torn Apart (Hero Series #1)
End Result (Hero Series #2)
Sole Intention (Intention Series #1)
Grave Intention (Intention Series #2)
Devious Intention (Intention Series #3) Due July 2016
Merry Widow (A Lorne Simpkins short story)
It's A Dog's Life (A Lorne Simpkins short story)
A Time To Heal (A Sweet Romance)
A Time For Change (A Sweet Romance)
High Spirits
The Temptation Series (Romantic Suspense/New Adult Novellas)
Past Temptation (available now)
Lost Temptation (available now)

Keep in touch with the author at
http://www.facebook.com/pages/Mel-Comley/264745836884860
http://melcomley.blogspot.com
http://melcomleyromances.blogspot.com

THE CALLER

PROLOGUE

The two teams left the flat and went their separate ways in the car park.

"Right, let's see who's first on our list. Only, you and me, my friend, are going to play things a little differently to what our leader wants." Tyler dug his elbow into Malc's ribs, and they both laughed.

"Sounds like a plan to me, bruv. Ain't no black gits gonna boss us around. Get dialling."

Tyler called the first number on the list. "Hi, is that Heather Moriarty?"

"Yes, that's right. Who's calling?"

"It's Donaldson's Courier Service. I have a package for you."

"Really? I'm not expecting anything. Who's it from?"

"Ah, I can't tell you that for security reasons, love. Can I drop round now and deliver it?"

"Well, I was just about to go out. I have to be at work in half an hour."

"I'm just around the corner. Two ticks, I swear. Then I can get an early day in for a change." Tyler winked at his mate.

"Go on then. You've got my address, yes?"

"I have. Just to make sure, run through it again for me."

The woman gave him her address and hung up.

Malc started the engine and set off.

Tyler grabbed the cardboard box they'd obtained from a bin outside a local supermarket and opened the car door. "Wait for the nod and then join me ASAP."

Malc nodded. "No worries."

Tyler and Malc walked up the concrete path to the woman's small terraced house. Tyler rang the bell and fixed a broad smile on his face as he waited. Malc pressed himself against the wall, out of sight of the doorway.

A woman with a phone held to her ear answered the door then beckoned him into the hallway. "Yeah, I'm leaving right now. No, I'm not hungover. I paced myself well last night, unlike some I could mention." She chuckled.

The woman hung up as Malc stepped into the hallway and slammed the door shut behind him.

Tyler pounced on the woman, placed one hand over her mouth, and grappled with her flailing arm. "Help me get her in there!" he ordered, nodding at the first door off the hallway.

Malc grasped the woman's legs. She kicked out violently as they bundled her into the small lounge. Tyler's hand smothered her screams. Once they were in the middle of the lounge, Malc released her legs. Tyler took a swing with his fist, connecting with her jaw.

Something crunched beneath his knuckles, and the woman dropped like a lead weight.

"Damn, you didn't have to hit her that hard, man."

Tyler clicked his fingers. "Let's get this joint searched. Grab anything upstairs that looks valuable and shove it in a pillowcase. I'll concentrate on the cupboards. Maybe she'll have a stash of money hidden somewhere down here."

Malc glanced down at the woman lying unconscious at their feet. "What if she wakes up?"

"Let me worry about her. Move it! I wanna be outta here in ten."

He heard Malc run up the stairs and start ripping the place apart, while he opened every cupboard and drawer he could find in the lounge. "Yes!" He thumped the air triumphantly—underneath a pile of napkins and candles he'd found a wad of notes. Fanning his face with them, he estimated there were at least a couple thousand pounds in the bundle.

The woman stirred, and he shoved the money in his jacket pocket. Rushing over to her, he picked up a cushion. Before she could move, he straddled her chest. Her eyes widened in horror as his smirk broadened. He unzipped the cushion, cast aside the stuffing then shoved the cover in the dazed woman's mouth. With one hand, he secured her arms above her head, and with the other, he began tugging at her clothes.

Malc appeared in the doorway. Through clenched teeth, he shouted, "What the fuck are you doing, man?"

"Having some fun before we leave."

"Jesus, that wasn't part of the plan! I didn't sign up for that kind of shit."

"Don't be a dickhead. Get me something to tie her hands with."

Malc rushed into the hallway, returned with a tea towel, and gave it to Tyler.

He looked at Malc as if he were mad. "You ain't got a clue, have you?"

"No, I ain't into this. I want no part of it."

"You'll do as I say."

"Or else what?" Malc sneered.

"I'll tell your missus about that teenager you're shagging on the side."

"Cool it, man. I ended that friggin' months ago."

"I ain't having a debate. If you don't agree, then fuck off and leave me to have my fun."

Malc surprised the hell out of him when he left the room and slammed the front door after he exited the house.

Tyler looked down at the woman, who was shaking uncontrollably beneath him. "Looks like this is your lucky day, bitch."

Relief flooded into her eyes. As though he'd flicked a switch, his anger erupted. Tyler pounded her with his fists, and her head swung from side to side with each blow. Eventually, her eyes fluttered shut, and her body went limp. Unsatisfied, he pulled a knife from his pocket, ran his finger along the cool edge of the blade, then slit the woman's throat. As blood gushed from the wound, he hurriedly pushed himself off the woman's body. Staring down at her, he dusted his hands together. Finally pleased with his accomplishment, he left the house.

CHAPTER ONE

The following day Duke was livid. "What the fuck is wrong with these guys? I give them one fucking simple task to do!" He checked his watch for the thirtieth time that morning.

As part of an initiation test, Duke had instructed the two teams to break into two houses and return no later than six the evening before. Over fourteen hours later, there was still no sign of one of the teams. He couldn't tell if Malc and Tyler were idiots or if they were trying to piss him off just for the fun of it.

Chris chuckled. "I knew they'd be crap the second I laid eyes on them. Too cocky."

Duke stormed across the room and grabbed the front of Chris's shirt. "When I want your fucking opinion, twat, I'll ask for it. Got that?" He shoved the gang member away. "This is about our rep, man. We need the extra members if we want to stay in control. We have no choice but to recruit."

Chris glared at him for a second or two.

Come on, you dumb shit. Duke got the impression he was about to be challenged and was desperate for a reason to punch someone in the face. He didn't want to lose his cool in front of the boys, but the pressure was mounting. He hated to think perhaps he wasn't the right man for the job.

Chris relented and turned away. Frustrated, Duke shoved him back.

The new recruits, Feral and Ace, watched on in silence. Even though they'd returned empty-handed after their task the night before, Duke was willing to give them another chance to show their worth. After all, they'd come highly recommended from one of his long-term friends and business associates. Dev was actually the one behind their most recent scam. He and Duke were the only members of the gang with the sufficient brain-power to implement the audacious plan. The computer genius had hacked into a popular mobile phone company's records and gained access to the names and numbers of hundreds of customers. Because of the company's tight security, the addresses were kept separate from the names and numbers. But Duke had hatched the plan for his men to pose as delivery drivers and call the account owners to confirm their address. Duke intended to specifically target the homes of females on the list, presuming they would be more inclined to shop online and give out their address with less suspicion than male occupants would.

Duke then ordered his new recruits, who worked in teams, to telephone the homeowners and ask specific questions to discover when their homes were likely to be empty. Then they had to prove their worth by robbing the properties. Duke struggled with that part of the plan—it wasn't in his nature to be nice to people, even if it was only a sham. But in the end, the recompense would far outweigh his feelings of discomfort.

Duke Mason had become a member of the Streetlife gang when he was twelve. Its notorious leader, Leroy Charles, had soon become a father figure to him. After being welcomed into the group, he'd started out as the gang's prime runner-cum-lookout, but with Leroy's guidance, he'd quickly worked his way up and became the leader's right-hand man. The duo had been an image of power and authority on the Bridge Estate in Brixton, until January, when a rival gang gunned Leroy down on Duke's thirtieth birthday. Despite Duke's soaring rage, the Streetlife members had looked to *him* for instruction. He swiftly had to fill Leroy's shoes to ensure the gang kept their reputation, image and comfortable lifestyle intact.

He'd confided in his closest friend, Dev, and between them, they had come up with this plan, which he anticipated would keep the money rolling in for years to come. The only problem left to conquer was finding decent recruits with the right nous. So far, Feral and Ace had failed in their task, and Tyler and Malc had taken off. That riled Duke more than anything—those blokes had set out to disrespect him. Of course, anyone trying that kind of shit would feel his wrath soon enough.

Duke raised an eyebrow when he heard a knock at the door. "Get that."

Chris sauntered across the small room and opened the door a few inches. He peered into the gap then threw the door wide open. "I don't believe it!"

Tyler and Malc barged past Chris and swaggered into the room. Tyler deposited a pillowcase on the glass coffee table and flopped into the low black leather sofa. A smug grin on his face, he flung his arm over the back of the sofa, while Malc stood off to the side, looking unsure of himself.

"Sorry we're late. The car broke down last night. Think this lot will make up for any misplaced concerns you might have had?" Tyler asked.

Duke tore open the pillowcase and tipped the contents onto the table. "What the fuck? You got *all* this from one house?"

"Yep! And this." Tyler plunged a hand into his jacket pocket, pulled out the notes, and fanned the money in front of him.

Duke snatched it from his grasp. "Shit! Have you counted it?"

"Two grand. Nice snatch, eh?"

"Very nice. The others came back empty-handed. What happened? Did the owner leave a window open or something?"

"Yeah, we watched her leave for work and then hot-tailed it round the back. She looked as if she was in a hurry, so I figured she may possibly have forgotten to close a window. I was right. We let ourselves in the back door, and well... you can see for yourself that's the result."

"You're in, both of you. Maybe you can take the other two boys under your wing and show them the ropes."

"Nah, that's your job, mate. Malc and I work as a team. We've grown up together, know how the other one works. I know for damn sure we wouldn't get the same results if we had to babysit those guys."

Duke laughed. "I hear ya, but answer me one thing. If you do so well on your own, then why d'ya wanna be part of Streetlife?"

Shrugging, Tyler looked at him. "Let's just say I need a little help putting the ideas together. If it wasn't for you and your mate Dev coming up with the plan in the first place, we'd be rolling on our own with no prospects, man."

Duke narrowed his eyes. "Ah, I get ya. Well, what can I say? You boys are in, and if you keep this up, you'll be a valuable addition to the gang. What d'ya say?"

"For sure, it's a no-brainer for us," Tyler replied. "And who knows, maybe you and I can have a one-to-one soon. I might have an idea about somethin' we can hit. Somethin' *really* worth the effort."

"Meaning what? What you got in mind?" Duke asked, intrigued.

Tyler winked and tapped the side of his nose. "I don't wanna lay all my cards on the table just yet. Wouldn't want you nicking my ideas now, would I?"

Duke enjoyed a challenge just as much as the next man, but there was something about Tyler he couldn't help admiring. The man's cocky nature reminded him of himself when he'd first joined up with Leroy. He bumped his clenched fist against Tyler's, then Malc's. "Welcome to Streetlife, boys. Do as I say, and you'll fit in nicely."

CHAPTER TWO

Angela North stood by the patio doors of her home, contemplating her life, not for the first time over the last few weeks.

"Penny for them?" Warren, her husband of sixteen years, came up behind her, slipped his arms around her middle, and kissed her neck.

"Eww... get a room, you two. That's gross at this hour of the morning," Luke complained as he dropped his backpack on the floor and pulled out a chair at the kitchen table.

She kissed her husband on the lips and snuck out of his grasp to attend to their teenage son. "Good morning to you too, darling. I'll remember that comment when you get a girlfriend."

"Yeah, right! As if, Mum," he grumbled, pouring a healthy glug of milk over his cereal.

Warren ruffled Luke's hair on the way over to the coffee pot. "I've seen the way the girls eye you up, mate. It won't be long before you're knee deep in invitations for dates."

Angie cringed, waiting for her son's moody exchange. He hated when his father ribbed him about the opposite sex.

Luke glared at his mother and jabbed a thumb in his father's direction. "Is he for real?"

"Maybe he's thinking back to the dark ages, to the time when we started out. I hate to tell you this, love, but the dating world has changed significantly since our day."

"It has? Who'd have thunk it?" Warren exclaimed, winking at Angie.

She shook her head and sighed. "If only life was as simple as deciding who to take out next, eh?"

"If only! What's wrong, Angie? Are you apprehensive about today?" Warren poured his coffee and leaned against the worktop.

"Not sure *apprehensive* is the right word. My heart is definitely pounding much harder than usual; that's for sure."

"You'll be fine. Just think of it as a fresh start."

"That's what I'm worried about. I'm totally in the dark where this team is concerned. You know how much familiarity in the workplace means to me. I'm too old to start anew. For all I know, this new team could be a bunch of intellectual idiots—you know the type, all brains and no common sense."

"I doubt it. But if they are, I'm sure you'll take pleasure in showing them who's in charge, love."

She sighed heavily. "Do I really want to start brandishing the whip at my time of life? I'd just managed to mould my last group into a team worth having, and then this promotion comes my way. It seemed a good idea to accept the new role when I was offered it. Now I'm not so sure; truth be told, I'm dreading it."

"First-day jitters. You wouldn't be human if you didn't have them. Anyway, these guys are supposed to be the cream of the crop, aren't they?"

"Yeah, you're right. I'm probably talking out of my arse. You've got that party on tonight, haven't you? That'll mean a late one for you, won't it?"

"Yep, I'm going in early this morning. The caterers are due around ten, and I've drafted in extra staff to cover the shifts during the course of the day. If we can pull this off, then it bodes well for the future. The accountancy firm we're catering for holds regular entertaining events for its corporate clients."

Angie rubbed her husband's arm and smiled lovingly at him. "Sounds fabulous. You deserve your success. No one can say you haven't worked hard to achieve it either, darling."

"I don't mind telling you that I think it might be taking its toll on me, babe. I'm in dire need of a holiday—we both are. Imagine the scene: the three of us relaxing on a deserted beach somewhere, under coconut palms…"

"Yeah, being bombarded by dozens of falling coconuts," Luke added drolly.

Angie laughed. "Ouch, I'd rather not. Those things can hurt. Maybe we can look at some brochures and book a holiday in the summer; it would make a change. You can delegate the running of the pub to Haden. You should have him trained up to your high standards by then, shouldn't you?"

"He's still young, prone to making immature mistakes, but improving daily. To be honest, today's event will be a test for him. I'll be there to supervise. However, I've told him that the majority of the work will be carried out by him."

"Wow, really? And what was his take on that?"

Warren gave a brief shrug. "He accepted the challenge. If I had any doubts about his ability to pull it off, I wouldn't let him loose on such a valuable contract. Let's hope I don't live to regret my decision."

"Looks like we're both going to have to dig deep to combat a fraught day ahead in that case. I better get a wriggle on. I want to be at the station before the others, to give the right impression from the off." She planted a kiss on Warren's lips. "Good luck, not that you'll need it. I'm sure Haden won't let you down."

"Best of luck to both of us. Probably see you this time tomorrow," he called after her when she left the kitchen. Luke was too involved in his computer magazine to notice her exit.

Her stomach muscles contracted as she parked the car in her allotted space and withdrew her briefcase from the backseat. Head held high, she marched into New Scotland Yard, Victoria.

She introduced herself to the desk sergeant, who arranged for a constable to show her upstairs to her team's office.

Angie wandered around the open-plan space, running her fingers over every surface. The ritual, which she did whenever she started at a new station, gave her an intimate feel for her surroundings. For some reason, though always carried out in private, it helped her to feel part of her team.

Sensing someone was behind her, she swiftly turned when she reached the end of the room. Heat rushed into her cheeks when she saw the amused grin on the face of her new DCI, Raymond Channing. "Oh dear, I've been caught in the act."

He chuckled. "Nothing like baring your soul to your new team commanding officer, is there, Inspector?"

"Sorry, sir. What can I say? It's customary."

He shook his head. "There's no need to apologise. We all have our own little habits, I suppose. I saw your car in the car park and thought I'd drop by and formally welcome you. Do you mind not having any personal space, an office of your own?"

"Not at all. I've always been a team player, so this layout suits me perfectly, thank you." She had taken to her DCI the minute she'd met him at the interview. He had gone out of his way to put her at ease. She hadn't found him stuffy in the slightest, unlike many other DCIs she'd had the displeasure of knowing.

"Are you looking forward to your new role and the challenges that lie ahead, Inspector?"

"Absolutely, sir. A little trepidation crept in during the drive over here, but now I'm here, in this office, I can't wait to get started."

"Have you met any of the team yet?"

"Not yet. I haven't even had any personal files to look through, so I'm just as much in the dark about them as they are about me."

"I thought maybe it would be a good idea if everyone started off on the same foot. I remember joining a team years back now, pretty much like this one really, where only the best in their field came together. From the word go, we all began as strangers. No one had the advantage of knowing anything about anyone's past, good or bad. I believe it assisted in forming a far stronger unit."

"I can understand your reasoning, sir. Let's hope the other members of the team feel the same way."

He nodded. "I thought we could get the team to introduce themselves one by one and spend the first half an hour or so getting to know each other before I hand over the first case."

While Angie thought his suggestion was a good one, she was intrigued to know more about the investigation he had lined up for them to sink their teeth into. "Good idea. What sort of case is it?"

"Briefly, a murder case." He raised his hand when she opened her mouth to ask another question. "I've said too much already. Let's do it my way for now, okay? After the initial meeting has finished, I'll hand over the reins and promise never to interfere with another investigation again."

Angie laughed. "Really? Can I get that in writing? Because you'd be the first DCI I've ever worked with who didn't attempt to involve themselves in any of my cases."

"You'll find I prefer to do things a little differently, Inspector. By all means, see me as a confidante but I've never enjoyed being the type to lay down the law about how I expect my inspectors to go about their business. You've earned your rank through your professionalism and ability. I recognise how tough it is for female officers in the force. However, I'm one of those who believe that women are just as competent as their male counterparts." He leaned in, cast an eye over his shoulder then said quietly, "In my experience, the women inspectors have been more mature than most of the men I've had under my command." He stood upright again. "When I hired you for this role, I had no illusions about what I was getting. I appreciate it when someone sticks up for their rights, the way you did with that harassment charge you had to deal with two years ago."

Angie's eyes flickered shut for a second, and she cringed. She had tried hard to put that personal case aside. Though she knew it would inevitably crop up now and again, it still touched a raw nerve when it did resurface. She prayed that this would be the one and only time her direct superior ever referred to it. "It's in the past, sir. I'd prefer if it remained there too, if you don't mind?"

The chief had the decency to look embarrassed by her request. "I completely understand where you're coming from, Inspector. I truly didn't mean to bring it up and cause you any unnecessary discomfort, and I would certainly never have discussed it openly in a room full of people. I just wanted to make you aware from the beginning of our working relationship how much I admire you for having balls. There, I've said it."

Angie dropped onto the edge of the desk behind her and placed her hands on her thighs as she laughed raucously. "I'll take that as a compliment, sir. I think you and I are going to get along just fine."

"I have no doubt about that, Inspector. Ah, I hear footsteps in the hallway. Maybe that's your team arriving."

"If it is, then I approve of their enthusiasm to show up early for their first shift."

"I concur."

A young man wearing a nifty grey suit walked into the office. "Hello, I guess I must be in the right place. I'm Tommy O'Brien." He shook the chief's hand then took a few paces to his left to shake Angie's.

"Pleased to meet you, Tommy. I'm Inspector Angela North, and this is DCI Channing."

"Sorry to ask, but what do you prefer to be called, ma'am? I know some women officers in charge get a little shirty about the subject."

"Definitely not ma'am. How about Angie? It's my name," she replied, smiling at the young man who seemed a little nervous in their presence. She was dying to find out more about him. He was handsome and very tall, at least six-foot-two. She thought she detected an Irish lilt to his voice but wasn't quite sure, although his name helped to cement the idea of his origin.

"Angie it is." He fell silent and looked around him.

She wanted to make him feel at ease. "Hey, as you're the first to arrive, you can have the privilege of picking which desk you want to claim."

Tommy chose the desk closest to the entrance, dropped into the chair, and clasped his hands in front of him. More footsteps approached, then a woman opened the door warily.

"Hello, there. Not sure if I have the right office or not."

Angie tilted her head. "What office were you hoping to find?"

"The Organised Crime Team office. Have I come to the right place?"

"You have. Come in and join us. I'm DI Angela North, and this is DCI Channing. You are?"

"Jill Alder, ma'am."

"Okay, Jill, welcome aboard. We'll wait for the other members to arrive before we go into details about the team. Grab a desk and make yourself comfortable."

Within a few minutes, the entire team had assembled. Everyone sat in silence with Angie and the chief standing in front of them. She cleared her throat. "Right, I'm glad to see you're all punctual, always a good trait to have when enrolled in one of my teams. I thought we'd break the ice a little by letting everyone introduce themselves. Do any of you know each other?"

They all shook their heads.

"To make it easier, I'll go first. I'd like to make it clear from the outset that I wouldn't expect you to embark on anything I wouldn't be prepared to do myself." She glanced at the chief and awaited his approving nod before she continued.

The chief smiled.

"I like to give my teams an insight into me as a person, what I expect from my work colleagues, and a little background of what goes on outside of working hours. I've been an Inspector with several police forces in the area. My last role was as a member of the Regional Investigation Team for the Special Operations Unit. So, in a way, this promotion is a sideways step for me, and one that I'm looking forward to being involved in. Our unit, the Organised Crime Team, has been created to work alongside the National Crime Agency, to tackle the threat from serious and organised criminals. As the OCT, our focus will be on the five main organised threats in London today: drugs, firearms, burglary and major robberies, immigration, and repeat offenders. I'm sure you'll all agree that having our base at Scotland Yard will be a huge benefit to us. It also means we're in the best possible place to work alongside some already outstanding established teams."

The team members nodded, then she continued, "I'm aware of the reputation we redheads have, and I want to assure you from the get-go that what they say is totally true. We do have very fiery tempers. I try to keep mine restrained wherever possible, but occasionally, it does emerge of its own free will. I apologise in advance for that." She chuckled. "If I stumble across any spare time in my life, I enjoy spending it with my family: my husband, Warren, of sixteen years—yes I really am that old—and my son, who is fourteen, although he tends to spend most of his time in the isolation wing most people normally call a bedroom. I don't have time for any real hobbies as such; however, I like to get away to Cornwall as much as possible. Lately, that luxury has become a rarity, due to my and my husband's busy work schedules. Warren runs a pub in the heart of London for his sins." Angie paused and looked around the room. She had the team's undivided attention. "I want to say how much I'm looking forward to working with you guys. Even though I know nothing about your backgrounds, I trust the chief's judgement explicitly in assembling this new exciting team. Now it's your turn to tell the group anything you feel comfortable sharing. The more we know about each other, the better we'll all get along, within reason of course. You can leave out the finer details of your sex lives if you don't mind. Who wants to go first?"

Without hesitation, Tommy raised his hand. "I'd like to do that, ma'am—sorry, I mean, Angie."

"Okay, I can tell you guys aren't used to calling a DI by their first name, so I'll leave it up to you what you call me, within limits of course." She smiled and then added, "I will say one thing though: yes, I'm a DI, and the final decision will always be down to me, but we're a team, and I would rather you all regarded me as your equal, okay?" Angie announced to the rest of the group. "Go ahead, Tommy. I'm interested to hear what brought you to our shores. You're Irish, right?"

"Yes, I'm from a large town in Kerry called, Tralee. I'm Tommy O'Brien. Umm... in a nutshell, my mother's suicide prompted my move. Sorry if that sounds too blunt. Of course, her death affected me deeply at the time, especially as my three siblings and I were abused by my father. He blamed us for our mother's death. He was wrong, by the way; the autopsy proved that she was riddled with cancer. She gave in to the disease. My thoughts are that she couldn't cope with the knowledge of going through months of chemo treatment and letting the nurses see the signs of abuse dished out by my father. Anyway, my siblings made allowances for my father's actions, but I couldn't. I just wasn't prepared to put up with his bullying ways any longer. So I moved to England when I was seventeen, worked three different jobs while I studied, first at college and then uni. I inherited my mother's determined streak."

"Sorry to interrupt your flow, Tommy—what course did you enrol in at uni?" While Tommy's heartbreaking story had moved her, Angie felt it best not to comment on what he'd revealed about his family.

"Computer science. I left uni at twenty-two with a degree and no prospects of getting employment in the industry, so rather than sit on my arse and dwell on that, I decided to see what opportunities were on offer down at the local job centre. I applied to be a police constable on the beat. After a few months, my sergeant saw an ounce of potential in me and urged me to apply for an opening which had cropped up in CID. The rest is history, so it is."

"Sounds like you'll be a key member of this group with your computing skills, Tommy. What do you like to do in your spare time?"

"If you're asking in a roundabout way if I'm single, yes I am. I suppose I just haven't met the right sweetheart willing to take me on yet."

"She's out there. No fear of that, Tommy. How old are you?"

"Twenty-six, boss."

"My advice would be not to rush into things. Enjoy life while you have the chance. Thanks for being so open with us." Angie's gaze drifted to the next desk. She pointed at the gentleman in his mid-thirties. "Would you like to go next?"

He shrugged, sat upright in his chair, and pulled his jacket over his slight paunch. "I'm Frank Delaney. I began my career with Surrey police and got promoted to DS fairly quickly. I remained in that particular job for around ten years." He gave an embarrassed smile.

Angie could tell he wasn't used to speaking publicly, so she prompted him, thinking a conversation might make him feel more comfortable. "Ten years as a DS, you must've been well thought of by your superior officer, Frank."

"I was. But I needed more of a challenge, so I opted to get more involved in the financial side of things and soon got promoted to a Financial Investigations Manager. My name is on a lot of paperwork to hundreds of fraud cases in the area. My main role was to achieve convictions against the fraudsters, delve into their finances, and deliver the evidence found at their properties to the courts. This is the part where I turn you against me," he said, grimacing. "I'm divorced and have a four-year-old daughter, who I treasure dearly."

"Why would that turn us against you, Frank? Divorce statistics are at an all-time high, aren't they?" Angie noticed Frank's hesitation to share his personal information with the group of strangers.

"Let's just say I made some wrong choices in life, boss."

Angie's eyes widened. "I see. Well, we're all guilty of that; it's whether we learn from those mistakes that really matters in this life," she said, chattier than normal because of her nerves.

Frank shook his head. "I'm remaining single for the foreseeable, boss."

She didn't bother to correct him calling her boss because she'd learned how stubborn some of the older members of her teams could be. "Right, who's next?" Angie's gaze drifted to the only other female member of the group.

The woman with short black hair and chiselled cheekbones smiled. "I don't mind. I'm Jill Alder. I've just turned forty, even though I feel like I'm still twenty-five. Although, I'm not sure my fitness would stand the test of time if I had to leg it after any criminals out in the field."

Angie laughed. She could tell she was going to get on well with this woman, and the rest of the team so far, for that matter. "I know that feeling. Maybe we'll leave that task to the boys, eh?" Angie smiled at Jill.

"I'm all for that, Angie. I'm married to Nathan, who runs his own accountancy firm. Sadly, we don't have any children, but on the other hand, it's probably a blessing in disguise as my parents are both in a care home; Dad has dementia and Mum is on hand to care for him. I'm a Certified Forensic Computer Examiner. I was a trainer with the Forensic Department before I got transferred to the Merseyside police. We decided to move south when Dad became ill. My parents used to work at the old Scotland Yard building, during their career in the force. It's hard dealing with what Dad has become, after living such a fulfilling life. That's all there is to know about me, really. All my spare time is spent visiting Mum and Dad, taking the strain off Mum a little. I could never be one of those kids who dump an ill parent in a care home and forget about them. He means far too much to me."

"I think I would feel the same if anything happened to my Mum and Dad, Jill. It's lovely to meet you. Who's next?" Angie asked the last two members of the team.

The younger of the two men raised his hand. "I'll go next if you like. Hi, everyone, I'm Scott Whitehouse. I'm twenty-eight and engaged to a beautiful woman called Liz. She's a catwalk model on the Milan, Paris, and British circuit; it sounds far more glamorous than it actually is. We're getting married in August and hope to start a family right away—she's desperate to get out of the business. I started my career working as an insurance broker with HSBC bank and spotted an advert in the *Evening Standard* for an opening in the fraud squad. I applied and was as shocked as everyone else in my family when I got the job. I have a younger brother, who sadly has a drug problem. When my fiancée and I are not organising our wedding, my time is spent desperately trying to help my brother kick his nasty addiction. I'm looking forward to working with you all and making a difference on the streets of London and the surrounding area."

"That's great, Scott. Congratulations on your forthcoming marriage, and I'm sorry to hear about your brother. That's a tough call."

"Thanks, Angie. We're getting there with him. I won't give up on him; that's for sure."

"And finally, you are?"

"Hello to you all. I'm Colin Bishop, aged thirty-six. I must be married to the most insane woman I know, because she's put up with me for so long." Colin laughed and the others joined in. "We've been trying for a baby since we tied the knot five years ago. This year, we're saving up to go down the fertility route with the help of our parents. I was educated at the City of London Police Economic Crime Academy and went on to become a DC in the Lewisham area, in the fraud squad. To be honest, I didn't find the role challenging enough, so when the opportunity cropped up to join vice, I jumped at the chance. I then became a drug specialist and have successfully brought down several of the largest suppliers plying their trade on the streets of London in the past few years. I have to say that I'm super excited to be involved in such a focussed group. I thank you." He bowed slightly as the team applauded each other's speeches.

Angie nodded and joined in. "You guys have just blown me away. I'm very proud to be associated with such an experienced team. I'm sure we're going to get on really well together. I'm going to hand over the reins to the chief now. He'll fill us in on our first task together as London's newest Organised Crime Team."

CHAPTER THREE

Angie admired the way DCI Channing addressed the team. All the DCIs she'd worked under in the past had communicated through her, with the intention of her relaying their instructions to her teams. DCI Channing was, therefore, starting off on the right foot in her eyes. She questioned whether he would maintain that work ethic.

"So, here's the deal, people: as soon as we had a starting date for this team being assembled, I began asking around the various squads in the area for any operations that were bothering them. You know the type of thing: crimes that they appeared to have problems solving or ones they didn't have the resources to throw at because of all the cutbacks. Well, surprise, surprise—two cases landed on my desk before the day was out. One I'm thinking about throwing back at the team who tried to pass it off, but the other one sounds a very intriguing case that I think we should tackle between us."

She frowned. "Between us? As in you'll be helping us solve the cases, sir?"

"No. Of course, I'll be there if you run into difficulties and need my advice, but it was a simple slip of the tongue, Inspector. I promise, no unnecessary interference on my part, unless you ask for it."

"That's good to hear, sir."

He smirked as he walked over to the whiteboard at the back of the room and picked up the marker pen lying on the small shelf. "We have two victims: Heather Moriarty, aged thirty-seven. She was found beaten to death in her home with her throat slit. Her case has been open for two months now, with very few leads. All former partners have been questioned and discounted once their alibis were checked out. The investigating team have been left scratching their heads and wondering where to turn next. Then another victim, with a similar MO, was discovered last month: Sarah Lincoln, twenty-three. Again she was found in her home beaten to death *after* she'd been raped."

"Horrendous. Do you think we're looking at a serial killer here, or is it perhaps gang related? Perhaps the perpetrators are escalating in their violence or altering their MO slightly to try and get the police off their scent?" Angie asked.

The chief shrugged. "I don't know. That's something we're going to have to find out, Inspector. The victims were also robbed, but I think if it was a 'basic robbery' we were talking about, there would be more clues to go on. I'm inclined to believe that we're dealing with something far more sinister and organised here."

"What about any similar features to the women? Is there anything there we can go on?" Colin asked.

The chief shook his head. "Nothing that stands out. The first victim was black, the second white."

"So, the only genuine similarities in the crimes are that both women were found at home and both were beaten to death." Angie cupped her chin between her forefinger and thumb and tapped her cheek with her finger.

"So it would appear," the chief replied.

"I take it house-to-house enquiries were actioned at both scenes?" Angie asked.

"Yes, and nothing untoward presented itself."

"Given that fact, are you saying that the investigation teams gave up?" Colin queried.

"I wouldn't necessarily put it that way," Channing replied. "I suppose they probably hit a brick wall and were at a loss where to turn next. Maybe a more important crime landed on their desk." Angie opened her mouth to speak, but he silenced her with a raised hand. "Don't shoot the messenger—it's just an assumption. I know that will never happen on this team."

Angie agreed with a swift nod. "So where do we start?"

"I suggest at the beginning. Requestion family and friends, even neighbours of both victims, and see what surfaces."

Angie nodded thoughtfully. "Do you know if the investigations went down those routes, sir?"

"I have no idea, Inspector. Maybe that's where your team should start."

"I'll take a good look through the file first and then decide."

"I think that would be best to treat this case, or cases, as if they've only just occurred and conduct your investigation fully from the outset," the Chief suggested. "Not that I'm saying the other teams haven't done that already. However, we all know the benefits of having another set of eyes look over a perplexing investigation. I'll leave all of you to get acquainted and dip your toes into the cases. You'll find my office along the hallway. Any problems, just drop by and see me. Obviously, go through the inspector here first."

The team nodded their understanding, and DCI Channing left the room.

Angie picked up the files and scanned a few pages of each case while the team watched her reaction. She shook her head several times and tutted. "Just a brief look tells me that there are holes in the investigation. Let me take a thorough look at the files, and I'll get back to you. In the meantime, if anyone has any form of contacts on the streets, snitches or the like, would you mind getting in touch with them to see what comes up?"

"I have a few. I'll put a discreet word out and see what response I get." Colin reached into his pocket and withdrew a small black notebook, which he flipped open to a page full of writing.

"Wonderful, let me know how you get on. Anyone else?"

"Not me, boss," Frank replied with a shrug. "I can look into the victims' financial backgrounds, if you like?"

"Okay, Frank, I want you to team up with Tommy and get that done. Jill and Scott, I'm unsure how much background knowledge we have about the victims in these case notes, but I want you to do your own preliminary research into them and see what you can find."

After reading the first page of one of the cases, she'd already made several notes. By the end of the morning, Angie had filled two full pages in her notebook and felt saddened that the original teams had given up so easily.

She called the team to attention and propped her backside on her desk. "Don't ask me why these cases have been screwed up, but it's clear after reading through both files that vital information wasn't chased up at the time. You know what that means: our job will be harder from the word go."

"How do you know the information was missed, Angie?" Jill asked tentatively, raising her hand.

"I noticed on the first case—that of Heather Moriarty—there was mention of someone who had seen a strange vehicle hanging around outside her house. That was the first and last time that piece of information was referred to. Had it been my investigation, I would've built an enquiry on that snippet of information."

"I agree," Jill replied. "That's shameful if it's true. Maybe the investigating officer simply neglected to note down the follow-up investigation because it bore no significance on the case. Do you want me to check with the officer?"

"Hang fire on that at the moment, Jill. I think there are a few things on my list we'll need to run past the officer concerned. I need to get my facts straight before I grab someone round the throat and shake the living daylights out of them."

"I understand. Such as?"

"Just general discrepancies, like not returning to a neighbour's home to take down a statement. Not applying for the victims' phone records to see if that could be deemed as useful. Basic things like that, which any experienced officer should organise without fail. I think it would be best if we ripped up the file completely and started afresh, with both cases."

Jill frowned and shook her head, condemning the officers. "Sounds like that would save us a lot of time in the long run. I'd certainly prefer to start from scratch, if as you say, there are significant inconsistencies. The last thing we should be doing is wasting a lot of time and energy being annoyed at their utter incompetence. If this team has been assembled because we've all excelled in our careers, then maybe this type of scenario is going to crop up frequently. We should decide now how we're going to deal with other squads' ineptness."

"I'm with Jill," Angie said. "If anything, I'd rather start over than pick through someone else's cock-ups. Right, do you want me to pair you up for these tasks, or would you rather do that yourselves? Oh, before you start teaming up, I'm going to plump for Tommy to partner with this time round." She stifled a laugh when an expression of bewilderment and fear crossed the young man's face. "Is that all right with you, Tommy?"

He gulped loudly. "Er... yes, of course."

Angie smiled. *I bet I can guess what he's thinking. Crap! Why have I been chosen to work alongside the boss over the others?*

The group quickly discussed the task and paired up. Frank and Colin would work alongside each other, while Jill and Scott formed another partnership. Angie was pleased with the decision—it meant each team had a financial expert, and she was blessed with the computer whiz.

"Okay, why don't two teams get out there and begin the house-to-house enquiries, while the other team remains here to conduct further in-depth background checks, chasing up the phone records et cetera, things that were missed on the initial investigation?"

"I'd prefer to stay here, if you don't mind, boss," Frank said, still insisting on calling her 'boss'.

"All right, that's settled then. We'll grab a quick bite to eat. Then we'll get cracking after lunch. Anyone know a good baker's in the vicinity?"

Tommy jumped up. "Want me to organise the sandwiches? I eyeballed a baker's down the road on the way in."

"Sounds good to me. I'll pay for lunch today. Call it a 'getting to know you' gift. Just don't expect me to do it every day," she said, jokingly.

CHAPTER FOUR

After they'd eaten lunch and washed it down with strong coffee, the team split up. Angie and Tommy drove to the first victim's address, while Jill and Scott headed over to the second victim's house.

"Have you got any ideas about the case yet, boss... sorry, Angie?"

"Not really, Tommy. What about you?" she replied as she parked near Heather's home.

"Nope. Let's hope we have more to go on at the end of the day. We're a solid team in the making, so we are."

Angie couldn't help but smile at the sound of Tommy's accent. Its genuine warmth appealed to her. "I think I have to agree with you there. I'll also add that from my point of view, it's going to be great working as part of a team again, rather than dishing out the orders all the time. I admire colleagues who are willing and able to work on their own initiative. The other way gets a little tedious after a while. Let's see what we can find out here. Do you mind taking notes?"

"Of course not. Is it all right if I jump in with a relevant question now and again?" he asked, his tone full of uncertainty.

"I expect it. We're partners in every sense of the word out here, Tommy."

They approached the house to the left of Heather's. An old lady opened the door after relieving it of several security bolts. Angie wondered if the woman had installed the locks before or after her neighbour's demise.

She flashed her warrant card at the woman. "Hello there, I'm Detective Inspector North, of the Organised

Crime Team, and this is my partner, DS O'Brien. Would you mind if we asked you a few questions?"

At first, the lady seemed puzzled by their intrusion, then thumbed to her left. "Is this to do with Heather?"

"That's right. My team have taken over the case, and we're revisiting all the witnesses from the initial enquiry."

"Ah, I see. I keep checking the news to see if you lot have caught the bugger yet. I don't mind telling you it's a grave concern for me, living next door to where someone was murdered. People have the right to feel safe in their homes, don't they? There are far too many crimes like this. Where will it all end?"

"Maybe it would be better if we came inside for a chat, Mrs...?"

"Davidson. Edna Davidson. You can come in, but not for long, as I have to go out for some groceries soon, before it gets dark." She opened the door and walked up the hallway ahead of them.

The smell of menthol hit Angie's nose the second she stepped into the warm living room. An elderly cat was lying on the floor in front of an electric fire with one glowing bar. The cat raised a weary head, let out a disinterested sigh, and curled up into a tight ball again.

"Someone's comfy." Angie pointed at the ball of fluff.

"She loves a bit of heat, that one. A bowl of food twice a day, and then she's back in front of the fire straight away. Right, I'm not going to ask you if you want a cup of tea because, to be truthful, I've run out of milk, hence the need to venture out on a shopping trip later. So, what can I do for you?"

"We wondered what you could tell us about the day the incident next door occurred. Did you see anything perhaps? Anyone unfamiliar hanging around?"

"No, dear. To be honest, I wasn't here the day it happened. It was my daughter's fiftieth birthday, and we had a little gathering at her place. You can imagine the shock I got when I learned of the tragedy. Nice girl she was. Very pleasant; never had a bad word to say. I tried to recall if I'd ever heard her complain about anyone or anything, but no, I never did. Who would do such a thing to a sweet human being like that?"

"We don't know, but we certainly intend to find out. Well, I'm glad you were away at the time, out of harm's way. I suppose you discussed the incident with your neighbours, am I right?"

"Yes, we nattered about it, more out of fear than anything. It's scary times we're living in, dear. We've all sworn to be more vigilant about things from now on. A couple of the younger men have even set up a neighbourhood watch scheme since it happened. I know it's too late for poor Heather, but I have to say, before the scheme began, I never slept a wink. Now, I sleep twenty winks out of the forty I'm supposed to grab at night."

"That's good news. I think neighbourhood watch schemes prove invaluable in certain areas. So glad it's reassured you about living here. It must've been a traumatic experience for you to deal with."

"It has reassured me, if only a little. I'm sorry I can't be of more help. I would love to have helped Heather get the justice she deserves."

"So, even before the incident, you saw nothing out of the ordinary in the street? Even a few days earlier, perhaps?"

"No. This room is towards the back of the house. The only thing I really hear is when the neighbours are arguing. This side, I mean"—she pointed at her other neighbours—"not poor Heather. I never heard a peep out of her. She really was the model neighbour."

Angie nodded. "Are the couple next door young or old?"

"Youngsters. They both work in the city. Got high-flying jobs, I believe. The arguments tend to flare up around ten in the evening most days. I've contemplated making a complaint to the local police station, but then I thought better of it. It's hardly a life-or-death situation like Heather's case, and look how that was dealt with."

"We're trying our best to make up for that mistake, Mrs. Davidson. Do you know where your neighbours work? Could you tell us where in the city?"

"I'm afraid not, dear. They've made it perfectly clear they expect me to mind my own business. I tried to strike up a conversation about poor Heather, and *she* flounced off, her nose pointed in the air. He's all right, never hangs around long enough to say hello. Not sure if it's me they hate or Treacle." She nodded at the cat. "I suppose she does tend to use their garden as a toilet more than her own."

Angie smiled. "We'll check out their details on the electoral register and have a word with them. What about the other neighbours? Did anyone else mention anything significant about that day?"

The woman thought for a second or two then clicked her fingers. "Sorry, bad memory, and it's been a few months since it happened. I remember Joyce Willis at number twenty-five said she was taking her dog, Rascal, for a walk on the day the attack happened. She mentioned that she saw a strange car parked up in the street. You might want to have a word with her, dear."

"We'll do that. You've been very helpful, Mrs. Davidson. Here's my card if you think of anything else after we leave."

The woman showed them to the door and pointed down the street to Mrs. Willis's house. "That one there, dear. Good luck." She closed the door behind them, and several locks secured it again as Angie and Tommy walked away from the house.

"I guess no one is getting in there unless they're invited," Tommy stated light-heartedly.

"It must be hard getting old and fearing the world. I bet Edna never envisaged living next door to a murder scene when she bought the house. Can't say I blame her for being extra cautious under the circumstances."

Angie knocked on the front door of the young couple Edna had mentioned, just in case they had a day off from work, but she got no reply. Tommy followed her across the road and knocked on Mrs. Willis's door.

Angie saw the curtain twitch. "If anyone knows what went on that day, it'll be this woman," she whispered out the corner of her mouth, and Tommy sniggered.

Within seconds, a chubby woman wearing an apron and a deep scowl opened the door. "Yes, who are you, and what do you want?"

Angie and Tommy flashed their IDs and introduced themselves. "I wondered if you could spare us five minutes of your time," Angie said.

"You want to speak to *me*? About what?"

"Heather Moriarty's death and what went on that day."

"Has that Edna been putting her foot in it again?"

Angie chuckled in spite of the woman's stern expression. "She might have mentioned in passing that you two discussed seeing a strange vehicle on the day Heather was murdered. Care to fill us in on what you remember? It's important, as the case has been passed over to our team, and we're determined to solve it."

"We'll have to talk here then. Rascal can't abide strangers coming in the house." As if on cue, Rascal started barking ferociously on the other side of the door. "Hush now, go in your basket." The dog stopped barking instantly. "Now, what do you want to know?"

"What type of vehicle it was. Whether you happened to see the registration number."

"No, I should have. I realised that once the car pulled away, but hindsight is a wonderful thing. It was a newish car. One of those gas guzzlers, as my son likes to refer to them."

"A four-by-four? Is that what you mean?" Tommy asked, jotting down the details.

"Yes, a black one. I couldn't tell you if there was anyone inside because I couldn't see in the car."

"Because you were too far away, or were the windows tinted black, obscuring your view?" Tommy asked before Angie could.

"That's it—they were black. Seemed rather sinister to me. Perhaps I should have thought more of it at the time. I simply didn't think anything as horrendous as that would take place on my doorstep. Terrible situation."

Angie took up the questioning. "It is, one that we're trying our hardest to get to the bottom of. Have you ever seen this car in the area before?"

"I've tried to recall that a number of times but keep coming up with the same answer—I don't think I have.

That kind of fancy car would stick out, especially around here."

"Okay, can you remember anything else? Did you see anyone either walking towards or getting in or out of the car?" Angie asked, more out of hope than expectation.

"No, I wish I could tell you differently. It must be so frustrating for you, not having many clues to go on. I wish to God I could be more help. I just don't have the answers you're looking for."

"Well, a small piece of information is better than no information at all, Mrs Willis. I'll leave you a card just in case something comes to mind."

The woman tucked the card into her apron pocket. "Do you think this was a one-off? Was poor Heather specifically targeted?"

"We have no idea at this point. Thanks for sparing us the time, Mrs. Willis."

"No problem. I hope you catch the bastard who robbed that poor girl of her young life."

Angie and Tommy walked away from the woman's house, then Angie paused at the gate. "I think we should split up and knock on every door. It's a long shot; however, if Mrs. Willis remembered the black vehicle, the odds on other neighbours in the street doing the same are far higher than we first thought. How about you take that side, and I'll do this? Any hint of promise, we give each other a call, all right?"

"Okay. Let's hope someone can pinpoint who was driving the car." Tommy walked across the road and started at the last house on his side.

Angie did the same with the house opposite. Most of the doors remained firmly shut, which caused her frustration level to spike—until she knocked on the fifth door. The elderly man inside, who supported himself with a walking frame, was willing to speak to her. She explained why she was there and asked, "Do you recall seeing a suspicious vehicle in the street that day?"

"Yes, love. I did. And I saw the young fella get out of the car. I think it was the passenger side, unless it was one of those foreign cars. No, it wasn't—come to think of it, the car had a UK number plate." His eyes lit up as he spoke. Angie sensed he was pleased with himself for remembering such a crucial detail.

"That's excellent news. Hold on." Angie rushed back to the gate and called across to her partner. "Tommy, here a sec." Her partner gave up on the house he was trying and ran across the empty street towards her.

"Sorry, I forgot to get your name, sir?" Angie asked, motioning for Tommy to take down the man's details.

"Eric Morgan. I've lived on this road since I was a little boy. Not much escapes me. I was surprised when I didn't get a visit from the police after all the fuss died down."

"What fuss? When the incident happened, you mean?"

"Yep. I told one of the constables in uniform what I've just told you, and no one came back to question me further. I shrugged it off, presumed someone had given the police all the info they needed to catch the criminal. I'm a bit surprised that you're still asking questions today, love."

"The case has been handed over to us. We've decided to start from scratch with our enquiries."

He winked at her. "In other words, you think someone screwed up."

Angie chuckled. "So it would appear. It's our job to rectify that. Would you be able to recognise this man?"

"In a line-up?"

"If necessary. I was thinking more along the lines of looking through some mugshots of people on our radar, living in the surrounding area."

"Depends. It was a few months ago, after all. I've lost the use of several hundred brain cells in that time," he joked. "I could give it a whirl, if you wanted me to."

"Can you give me a rough idea what this man looked like?"

"He was young, white, athletic type, I seem to recall. I think he had some kind of tattoo on the side of his neck."

Angie and Tommy exchanged glances. "That could be relevant. Any idea what the tattoo was, or were you too far away to see it in detail?"

"Sorry, too far. I just saw the large blob of ink on his neck. Thick neck, he had, if that helps."

Tommy looked up from his notetaking. "Do you think he lifted weights?"

"Maybe, I wouldn't like to lead you up the wrong path by suggesting that. He gave me the impression he was a lean, mean fighting machine, if that helps."

Angie smiled. "Well, that will definitely help. Thanks, Mr. Morgan. Did you see him go in the house?"

The man tutted loudly. "I've just realised that he was carrying something in his hand."

"Such as?"

Eric closed his eyes. "A box. A small package."

Angie's interest was piqued. "So he could've been some kind of delivery man?"

"Driving that kind of car? Do they usually make deliveries driving swanky cars?"

Angie's mouth turned down at the sides. "Maybe his regular vehicle was off the road and he was using his personal one to make the deliveries. It's something we haven't come across before, so we'll definitely be chasing it up."

"You do that. Well, don't let me stop you from catching the killer. That's as much as I can tell you, love."

"Believe it or not, sir, I think you've given us more to go on than we had when we set out this morning. That's a bonus for us. Thank you."

"Will you get on the TV and radio now, asking for help? I didn't see much of that when all this was initially investigated. Thought that was appalling at the time."

"Definitely. That'll be our next job, to refresh the public's memories of the case. We'll throw in there what you've told us about the delivery side of things and the fact the man had a tattoo. Is it worth you coming down the station to look through our possible suspect lists?"

Eric shook his head. "I'm not very good on my feet any more, love. But if you want to bring me some photographs, I'd happily have a look. I can't promise anything, mind you, not after all this time."

"You've been very gracious with your time and information. We're grateful. If we have something we think worthwhile for you to look over, we'll be in touch." Angie led Tommy out the man's gate. They proceeded to knock on several more doors on both sides of the road, but the homeowners either weren't at home or chose not to answer the door.

In the car, Tommy sighed. "Let's hope we can track down this man, although do you have any idea how many bruiser types are walking the streets nowadays brandishing a huge tattoo?"

"Tons, I know. Perhaps mentioning it in a press conference will urge a partner or former partner to grass on the culprit."

"Maybe. Because we've got very little else to go on at the present."

"Which is a frustration in itself. Let's get back to the station, see if the other team has been more successful finding anything about our second victim."

Angie was excited to see Jill smiling when they entered the office. "I hope you're going to share some good news with us."

"Let's say it's mixed."

Angie perched on the desk closest to Jill's and leaned forward.

"After knocking on several doors and virtually having them shut in our faces, we finally had success with an old lady who appears to be some kind of neighbourhood watch person, although she wasn't at the time. Sarah Lincoln's death forced her into taking more interest in what's going on in her neighbourhood now," Jill explained.

"Interesting. That's exactly what the neighbours on Heather's street have done. Go on."

"She thought she saw a man approach the house with some kind of package."

Angie nodded. "Well, that rings true with what we have heard from an eyewitness too. Anything else?"

"The man was heavyset, and she thought, but she wasn't positive, she saw some kind of tattoo on his neck."

"Yep. I think we should check our records, see if anyone, or how many criminals, we can match that particular detail to. I think it's time for a press conference. I know we don't have much to tempt the public into confiding in us, but we have more than before. That's a big positive to me. Anything else?"

"Do you want me to check with the rest of the team first? Someone might know this character, saving us the job of trawling through all the files in the system. You know how time consuming that can be."

"Great idea. In the meantime, I'll organise the conference for tomorrow."

CHAPTER FIVE

Duke summoned the gang early, but true to style, Tyler and Malc strolled into the flat late. The annoying pattern was beginning to claw under Duke's skin. He had a dilemma. Granted, the pair had done well in their heists so far, and he was alarmingly aware of the need to uphold Streetlife's reputation. Still, after only a few months, he found their lack of urgency infuriating. But he needed to put his plans into action; too much time had passed. He would have to stick with them now, knock them into shape, and make sure they knew who was boss.

He stormed across the room towards them. "You're late," he snarled.

Tyler shrugged nonchalantly and chewed his gum noisily.

Duke's eyes narrowed as his temper rocketed. "Don't disrespect me. Sort your shit out or fuck off—the choice is yours."

Malc jabbed Tyler with his elbow. "Cool it, man."

"We had car trouble again on the way over here. There's no need for you to start threatening us. If you want us out, we'll take our skills elsewhere. No problem!" Tyler crossed his arms in defiance.

Duke wanted to punch the arrogant tosser in the face, but knew he had to remain calm in front of his boys. That much he'd learned from his predecessor and mentor. "Whatever. The choice is yours. I'll tell you this, though: I ain't about to sit around and be taken for a mug by you. Got that?"

"Like I said, the car was playing up. All right, I should've rung and told you we were gonna be late, but I was caught up with the repairs. My bad. What have you called the meeting for anyway?"

"Don't question me! You do your job, and I'll do mine."

Tyler glared at him. "Seems to me the only ones around here doing anything most days are Malc and me."

"Don't push your luck!" Duke bellowed, leaning into the man's face.

Tyler raised his hands in front of him. "Whoa, what is this? We're the ones bringing home any real catches lately, and you're jumping up and down on our chests for being ten minutes late. Why all the grief?"

"You have a lot to learn. Answer me this: do ya have a hard time with me being the boss around here?"

Tyler's brow furrowed. "No, you make it perfectly clear who the boss is every friggin' day. Why? Do you feel threatened?"

Duke laughed and tilted his head back. "You're kidding, right?"

"Simple question. That's how it's coming across to me. I'm not used to being put on the naughty step for being late or being expected to clock on and off. I'll remember that when we're called out to do a job in the middle of the night, man."

Duke clenched his fists as the rage bubbled deep inside him. "Quite the smartarse, ain't ya?"

"Nope! But maybe you should've drawn up some kind of contract from the start, then we'd all know where we stand."

He turned his back on the men and sauntered over to the window. Living in a high-rise tower block in Brixton had its perks. The Shard and Gherkin dominated his view of London's skyline and glistened under the sun's rays.

They called to Duke like beacons, and he yearned to be part of the capital, with the money to support his status. The scene calmed him. "Get out then. Both of you."

"What?" Tyler shot back.

Duke glimpsed the first shake in the man's resolve, and he grinned. "I ain't got time for brazen games. I don't owe you nothing, so leave." He turned to face Tyler, his jaw set tight.

"Easy, man. *You're* the boss—I know that."

Duke glowered at Tyler one last time before turning back to the window. "Right, enough of this shit then. Back to business. Dev, run through what's expected of the boys today, will ya?"

Dev reached for a sheet of paper on the coffee table and told the boys to take notes as he read out four names and numbers. "We want you to hit two houses each. We've upped the quota for today. Any problems?"

Tyler sighed. "Oh, come on, man!"

Duke spun round. "Another problem?"

This time, Tyler hesitated. "It's just... how come we get all the dirty work, and you guys sit on your arses around here?" He pointed around the room, starting with Chris, then Dev, and ending with his finger trained on Duke.

He grabbed Tyler's finger and bent it back. "You've got balls."

"Ouch, man! Let go! I thought it was a fair question."

Duke released his grip but was pleased to see Tyler refused to make eye contact with him.

"Admit it, you're all thinking the same thing, ain't ya?" Tyler asked, peering at the other three new recruits.

They remained silent. Their gazes shifted nervously between Duke and Tyler, and Duke was confident his slight outburst had unnerved them too.

Duke sniggered. "Looks like you're on your own there. These guys know when to keep their mouths shut."

Tyler's eyes widened in anger as he stared at the other men.

"Right, you've been given your tasks for today. Get out there and make me some money."

The four men left the flat without uttering another word.

* * *

"Thanks for backing me up in there, guys. That's the first, and last time, I speak up for us all. Do your own fucking dirty work from now on. If you want him and his cronies to shit on you from a great height, then you're going the right way about it." Tyler jabbed a thumb at his chest. "I ain't gonna allow that to happen again, no *way*. Be prepared for a falling out by the end of the week, 'cause I'll only let him push me so far before I deck him."

"I don't get it, man. If you feel like that, why do ya stick around?" Feral scratched his head, looking puzzled.

"It suits me to stick around. I'm biding my time." Tyler grinned mischievously.

Feral pulled on Ace's arm. "Come on, we better get outta here. He'll be watching our movements from the window."

Tyler smiled and shook his head. He walked over to his own vehicle and slipped into the passenger seat while Malc got behind the steering wheel. "Dumb shits! They ain't got a clue. But they soon will have if they keep coming back empty-handed. Duke ain't gonna allow that to happen for much longer."

"A word of warning, mate. Duke's anger is brewing because you challenged him. I'd be wary if I were you. You know about his reputation."

"Yeah, I know what it *used* to be, but he's not so hot now he's in charge, right? Would he have let me push him that far in front of the gang, with a little finger bending, if he was confident in his role? If I was in his shoes, I would've kicked my ass out the door the second I opened my mouth."

"You're skating, mate, and the ice is getting thinner every time you guys meet. Just saying!" Malc shrugged and started the engine.

"Hey, don't worry about me. I'm used to skating on thin ice. My skates are always razor sharp and ready for action." Tyler slapped his mate on the shoulder, tipped his head back, and laughed raucously. Once he'd ran out of breath, Tyler cleared his throat and dialled the number Dev had given him.

A woman answered on the third ring. "Hello?"

"Ah… Mrs. Dyer. It's Highgate Couriers here. I have a parcel for you. We tried to deliver it earlier in the week, but there was no answer."

"That's strange. I'm not expecting anything."

"I have a driver in the neighbourhood at the moment. I could arrange a redelivery for you."

"Well, I'll be home for another hour, but then I must go out."

"No problem. He'll be with you in the next hour."

"That's great, thank you."

"Could you just confirm your address for me, Mrs. Dyer?"

"13 Broughton Drive, SW9 0LC."

"Thank you."

Tyler ended the call and gave Malc the thumbs-up. "Sorted, mate! She's only at Broughton Drive, not far from Electric Avenue. Get going. Jesus, how easy was that to get her address? Stupid cow."

"You're gonna behave with her, ain't you, mate?"

"We'll see. If she plays ball with me and gives me what I want. That's up to her." He thumped Malc's arm. "You worry too much."

"Yeah, I have to bloody worry—you're a psycho at times," Malc grumbled.

Tyler reached into the backseat and picked up the dummy parcel he would use to gain entry to the woman's home. Malc drove up the quiet residential street, a stark comparison to the busy marketplace less than a mile away, and parked opposite number thirteen. "Straight in-and-out job. Get the stuff and tie her up, yes?"

"We'll see." Tyler hopped out of the vehicle, pulled his jacket collar up over his neck, and strolled across the road, checking the area for any witnesses as he walked. There weren't any. He rang the doorbell and turned his back. When the front door opened, he faced a woman wearing a pink towelling robe and a towel wrapped around her head.

She clutched the opening of her robe at the chest and smiled. "Sorry, just got out of the shower. I didn't think you'd be *that* quick."

"No problem, love. There's a little excess postage to pay on the package. Sorry about that."

"What is it? Can I see who it's from?"

Tyler moved towards her with the package then shoved it forcefully into her chest. The woman stumbled backwards into the hallway. He rammed into her, swiftly placing a hand over her mouth before she could scream. Tyler left the door open for Malc to join him. He tussled with the wide-eyed woman and thrust her into the kitchen at the back of the house. "I'm warning you, the more you struggle, the worse your punishment will be. Got that?"

Tears streamed from her eyes, and she nodded slowly.

The front door slammed behind Malc as he marched up the hallway to join them. "Hey, man, ease off a little."

"Shut the fuck up, moron. Give me the rope."

Malc reluctantly fished in his jacket pocket and removed the blue nylon cord. Tyler manoeuvred the woman into a position where Malc could gain access to her wrists.

"Hurry up!" Tyler urged, his gaze drifting to take in his surroundings, searching for possible valuables and hiding places.

"I'm going as quickly as I can. There. Done."

"Okay, get a rag or something and shove it in her mouth to shut her up."

The woman objected and pleaded with the men not to harm her. Malc removed the tea towel from the oven door handle and wrapped it around the woman's face rather than stuffing it in her mouth as Tyler had suggested.

"Soft shit! Right, leave her here and start tearing this place apart."

The men ignored the woman's muffled whimpers as they opened every cupboard and drawer in the kitchen before continuing through the house. Tyler spotted the woman's handbag in the lounge. He tore it open and searched her purse. He whistled when he discovered the purse bulging with notes and five credit cards. He pocketed the haul and moved upstairs with Malc. They split up on the landing, and Tyler took the main bedroom. He entered the room and immediately opened the sliding wardrobe door. From the top shelf, he removed numerous shoe boxes, all bulging with bank and credit card statements. Not what he'd hoped to find. Frustrated, he tipped the contents onto the floor and stamped on them. Then he returned to the wardrobe and tossed aside the woman's clothes. Again he found nothing of value lurking inside.

"What have you got? Anything?" he called out to Malc in the spare room.

"Nothing much. Just a load of boxes with books in them."

"What kind of books? Any expensive looking ones? They can be worth a bob or two."

"No, just a bunch of diet cookbooks and lovey-dovey crap."

"Damn! Okay, let's head out." Tyler stormed downstairs and into the kitchen. He ripped the tea towel off the woman's face and placed his head inches from hers. "I'm gonna ask you this once and once only. You give me the run-around, lady, and I'll make you regret your actions. Got that?"

The woman's breath caught in her throat, her hands shook, and her eyes grew even wider as she nodded.

"Where are your valuables?"

She began to sob.

He slapped her hard around the face. "Stop whining and answer the question."

Between the sniffles, her voice faltered. "I'm sorry, I don't have anything of value. I've just moved in."

That explains why there are so many unpacked boxes. "Jewellery! Where's your jewellery box kept?"

"I don't have one. This house was more expensive than I realised. The moving costs wiped me out. All I have is what's in my purse. I had to pawn my jewellery. Honest!"

Exasperated he lashed out at her again, cutting her lip where his hand made contact.

Malc latched on to Tyler's arm. "No, not any more. Let's leave it, mate. Take her word on it."

"Stop being such a wimp. Can't you tell when a bitch is lying to you?"

"I'm not! I swear I'm telling the truth. In my purse is all the money I have. Please, you have to believe me."

Tyler leaned down into her face again. "Don't tell me what I *have* to do." This time, he punched the side of her head, ensuring he got his point across.

Malc tutted. "Ease off, man. We should go, move on to the next one."

"We go when I say so. I need to have a little fun with this bitch first."

"Jesus, man, don't be such a dickhead. Leave her. Don't kill her like the others."

The woman gasped and struggled in her chair, trying to break free from her constraints.

"Fuck off! Now look what you've done—you've spooked the wench. Get outta here and leave us to have our fun."

Malc glanced at the woman and shrugged. "Do what he says, love, if you know what's good for you."

The woman gulped noisily, and her lip quivered. "Don't leave me alone with him, I'm begging you."

Malc's shoulders slumped as he left the room and walked towards the front door. Tyler watched the last glimmer of hope drain from the petrified woman's eyes as his associate left.

"No one likes the sound of begging. Let's see what valuables you're hiding beneath this." He snarled and tore open the woman's robe, exposing her naked body.

She screamed and kicked out at Tyler, catching him in the shin. After another swipe across her face, he yanked her out of the chair and threw her onto the kitchen floor. She tried to fight him off, kicking and biting where she could, but his fists connected hard and fast with her head and her body. She couldn't sustain the onslaught for long and soon lost consciousness.

Pushing himself off the woman's body once he'd finished abusing her, Tyler zipped up his jeans. He kicked her in the stomach and the side of the head then left the house. *There's no way she'll survive that beating. On to the next one.*

CHAPTER SIX

Angie had trouble sleeping that night, going over the cases again and again in her mind. The constant tossing and turning drove her husband to grumble, so she gave him an apologetic kiss and went downstairs to make herself a coffee. She took the steaming cup into the lounge, along with a notebook and pen. But when Warren entered the room at seven the following morning, all she had managed to write down were the victims' names. Angie was left wondering why her usually active imagination refused to spark into life with this case.

"What's wrong, love?" He sat down beside her on the couch, pecked her on the cheek, and flung an arm around her shoulders. "Sorry for getting shirty. I needed my sleep after a hectic day at work yesterday."

"It wasn't your fault; it was mine. I don't know what's going on with me. Maybe I'm struggling to work with the new team."

"Really? You've only been with them one day, love."

"I know. Maybe it's easy to use that as an excuse for my inability to crack the case." She snuggled into his shoulder and placed her feet on the chair beside her.

Warren slapped her shoulder and tutted. "Why do you always do that?"

Angie leaned away from him and frowned. "Do what?"

"Always put yourself down like that."

"I wasn't aware that I did."

"Well, I'm telling you that you do. If you were as crap as you think you are, then you wouldn't have gained the promotions you've had over the years or been tasked with your new role. So cut it out, right?"

She saluted her husband and kissed his lips. "Genuinely, I'm sorry for being a whinging cow."

He laughed and hugged her to him. "Now, did I call you that? No. All I said was cut out all the self-doubting that you throw around. You know you crack more cases than the average DI. Just don't be too hard on yourself when things don't always go according to plan. Hey, you only began the case yesterday. No one, least of all your DCI, is expecting you to nail these bastards by the end of the week."

"You're right. It would be nice, though. Wow, what a way to impress the new boss."

Warren laughed. "You're nuts. Are you setting off soon?"

"Yeah, five minutes more cuddling up to my honey, and then I'll hit the shower. You haven't really said how your day went yesterday. Was it successful?"

"Let's just say it could have been better. Haden was way out of his depths. I need to do some intensive training with him about keeping to a schedule. His timings were all over the place. You know how important it is to stick to a routine. He was finishing half a job and moving on to the next one. I had to pull him up early in the afternoon and tell him to slow down. If I hadn't, I reckon he would've wound up in hospital, having a breakdown."

"Poor lad. You think it's too much too soon for him?"

"I'm getting that impression. Maybe it's the youth of today. They expect everything handed to them on a plate and haven't learned how to think for themselves. Problem solver, he ain't."

"That's a bit harsh, love. What is he? Twenty-two?"

"Nope, try twenty-five. When you think back to when I was his age, I was already engaged to you and working as a bar manager in my first pub. That's a stark contrast to Haden's path. I thought he had some nous about him, but fear I misjudged his enthusiasm. He talks the talk. However, when it comes to the crunch, he seems to be one of those guys that are unable to work on their own initiative. I was hoping to grab some time for myself this year, but by yesterday's display, that daydream seems miles away."

"Not everyone can be as together and efficient as you, sweetheart. Maybe sit him down today and go through the day, hour by hour, pointing out *nicely* where he went wrong and see if that makes a difference."

"I thought of doing that, but at the end of the day, love, I need someone I can trust to run the business in my absence. I really didn't see any form of leadership qualities to satisfy my needs. I'll have a word, maybe throw it back to him and ask him how he felt things went. How's that?"

"It sounds like a good plan to me. What was his reaction when you started pointing things out to him?"

"He shrugged a few times as if he didn't care."

"That might have just been for show. Perhaps deep down, he was just embarrassed about letting you down after you'd shown so much faith in him. Rather than jump on him first thing, go in there all bright today and see if he approaches you first wanting to go over how the day panned out. If he doesn't refer to yesterday at all within the first hour or so, then call him into the office for a chat."

"Is that how you would go about it?"

"I would if I had an office I could call my own," she replied jovially, thinking of the layout of her new workspace. "I'm sure everything will work out in the end. Just don't be too hard on him. Let him see the error of his ways rather than you pointing them out. He's not daft; otherwise, you wouldn't have given him the opportunity to run the show yesterday. Just be thankful that you were on hand to sort things out before they went belly up."

"You're amazing! Have I told you that lately?"

"No, I think you might've forgotten that particular attribute of mine for a while. Right, I better jump in the shower."

He squeezed her for a second or two then pecked her on the nose before letting her go. "Remind me to tell you how amazing you are more often."

"Oh, I will. Don't worry about that."

Angie left the house an hour later and pulled into the car park just as Tommy was getting out of his old, Ford Focus, which was at least ten years old. He waved and walked towards her. Nodding his head in the direction of his ride, he said, "She's seen better days, but she's reliable. I can't bear to trade her in."

"I had a reliable car like that once, a mini. Had to get rid of her when I started going out with my hubby. Not enough leg room in the back, if you know what I mean."

Tommy's cheeks flared up with colour. "Umm... thanks for that, boss. I'll have that image of you and your hubby making out running through my mind all day now."

"Get away with you. I bet that's tame to what you get up to with your girlfriend." She raised a hand when he opened his mouth to speak. "It wasn't a hint. I'm not some kind of perv, I promise. Oh wait, when you told us all about yourself, you said you're single. Sorry if I've made you feel awkward."

"You haven't. You've got a good memory. Are you telling me that you remember every little detail about what each member of the team said?"

"Not every little detail, but enough, I suppose. You're all fascinating characters, and I'm looking forward to getting to know you all better. The early signs are that we're going to make a fab team. We better get a move on. I have a conference to prepare for this afternoon."

They walked into the station. Angie punched in the security code and entered the door leading through the newish building. When they arrived in the open-plan office, they found Jill already at her desk, the office phone wedged between her ear and her shoulder while she jotted down information. Angie removed her coat and poured herself a coffee from the thermos, in the hope that Jill had made a fresh pot when she arrived. By the time she turned around, Jill had hung up and was sitting back in her chair, a concerned expression darkening her features.

"What's wrong, Jill?"

"Well, I can't be sure, but I think we might have a possible link to the cases we're looking into already."

"A link? Meaning what?"

"I've just been informed that a young woman was beaten and left for dead in her home. Her friend had arranged to go out with her and turned up at the house to find the door ajar. She walked into the kitchen and found a Maxine Dyer lying on the floor, her hands bound behind her. She was unconscious."

"Crap. And where did this happen? Is that what makes you think there's a possible link?"

"Yes, well, that coupled with the fact that the woman was attacked in her home and her friend said it looked like a burglary. It raised an alarm bell with me anyway."

"I see. Okay, let's get a team out there this morning, start door-to-door enquiries, see if anyone saw some kind of deliveries going on in the area. Is Maxine still unconscious?"

"Yes, she was taken to Kings College Hospital, where she remains in a stable condition."

Angie winced. "Any signs of sexual assault?"

"I'm afraid so, yes."

"Jesus! Okay, let's work fast this morning on getting as many facts as we can about this attack. If we can get all the details together by two p.m., I can add this case to this afternoon's conference. Jill, can you ring the hospital? Ask what the state of play is there. Also, ask them to inform us when the woman gains consciousness."

"I'll do that now." Jill picked up the phone.

Angie looked up at the clock on the wall. It was still only eight thirty, and the morning had already started off with a bang. "I want you to stay around here with me today, Tommy. As soon as the other team members arrive, I'll send two of them out to conduct the enquiries. Can you do a background check on the victim for me? Let's make sure we're dealing with the same perps. You never know; there might be an angry ex on the scene we don't know about. The fact this woman is still alive is waving a red flag at me."

"On it now, boss. Maybe her attacker was disturbed in some way during the assault," Tommy suggested.

"It's a possibility."

Angie sat at her desk, sipping her coffee, until the rest of her team arrived. Not giving Colin and Scott a chance to take their coats off, she instructed them to set off to Maxine Dyer's address. "I'm presuming the Scenes of Crimes Officers will be at the house when you arrive. Just have a chat with them first, see if there's any indication of any DNA at the woman's house."

The two men left the office, promising to contact Angie immediately if anything useful came to their attention. She placed the calls to all the TV stations and the major press offices, letting them know about the conference. Most appreciated her call and explained they would gladly attend if it helped get the word out about the heinous crimes. Angie was left with a good feeling about what lay ahead of her. *If only Maxine Dyer could pull through and give us a formal ID of the attacker.*

When Colin and Scott arrived back at the station close to midday, the team gathered around to hear what they had to say. Colin flipped open his notebook. "SOCO were at the scene and said they'd managed to locate some DNA where Maxine's body was found in the kitchen. They're going to rush the tests through for us."

"That's great news. Hopefully, they'll come up with something we can work with to track this bastard down. What about the neighbours? Anything there?" Angie asked, sitting back in the chair with her arms folded.

Scott held out his hand and motioned in an unsure gesture. "Nothing concrete, but two neighbours remember a man approaching the victim's front door. One of the older neighbours said he had seen a man approaching the house with a parcel but thought nothing more about it and got back to tidying up his garage."

"Great. Did he see the man leave? Could the neighbour identify him in a possible line-up perhaps?"

"Negative on both counts, boss. I asked, but the old man said he'd rather not get involved as he didn't really know the girl. Looks like she was new to the area."

Angie sighed heavily. "Hmm… and yet it seems like the same offenders who beat her up and left her for dead possibly made their first mistake. I don't suppose you asked if the delivery driver had any identifying features."

Scott nodded. "There was a young female witness, in her late teens. She was reluctant to say much but confirmed the delivery man had a tattoo of some sort on his neck. The design wasn't clear, as she saw him from her window across the street. She didn't want to comment any further and seemed scared."

"Well, we can't ignore the gang presence and crime rate in Brixton. Local people may well live in fear. But at least we know we're dealing with the same culprit as the previous attacks. That'll save us a lot of time. Did anyone come up trumps on the tattoo yesterday? Is anyone still waiting for one of their contacts to get back to them?"

"I'm still waiting for one of my keen eyes on the street to get back to me," Colin said. "He was going to make some discreet enquiries. If anyone knows who this guy is, it'll be him. I probably won't hear until later on this afternoon. He's not exactly an early riser."

"Keep putting in the call to him, Colin, if you will. The sooner we can get a name for this 'menace'—I use the term loosely—the better. Did any of the witnesses mention the vehicle? A number plate we can chase, perhaps?"

"Yes, at least part of one. I'm going to search the system now. My guess is the plate's false. If they're pulling up outside victims' houses in broad daylight, not bothering if people note down their registration or not, then they must have something up their sleeves."

"Do we know if there was one attacker, or did he have an accomplice waiting in the vehicle?" Angie asked.

"Conflicting reports, I'm afraid," Colin continued. "The elderly neighbour said the man got out of the vehicle via the driver's side, while the teenager said the passenger side."

"Ugh… don't you despise it when that happens? How difficult is it to say left or right of the vehicle? Never mind. We need to chase our contacts on the street and the leads we have so far. These crimes seem to be connected, and the culprits are getting a taste for it. Not sure how they're likely to react once word gets out that the latest vic survived."

Jill joined the conversation. "Maybe it would be best if you left that fact out of the conference."

"I'm in two minds about that," Angie replied. "Pointing out they screwed up might send them in a spin, force them to act out of character. That way, it might raise more people's suspicions, which will inevitably lead to a prompt arrest. Am I wrong?"

Jill twisted her head from side to side. "It might also encourage them to try and finish what they started with our latest victim. I'm not sure. Have you had experience along these lines before?"

"You have a point, Jill. But either way, we'll ensure Miss Dyer is protected. Actually, can you confirm that there is a uniformed guard at the hospital with her? Also, if the number plates are fake, could the culprit be dropping us false clues with that? We need to find out!"

"I agree. It's a tough one to call, boss. I'll kick my contact up the arse, see if that brings forth a name," Colin interjected. He turned back to his desk and pulled out his mobile.

Angie secretly crossed her fingers that he would manage to obtain a name.

Before long, Colin returned to the team, wearing a broad grin. "Eureka!"

"Don't keep us in suspense," Angie urged, her heart thumping against her ribs.

"Streetlife."

Angie wrinkled her nose. "Is that supposed to mean something? Only it doesn't, not to me anyway."

"The Streetlife gang. A notorious outfit in the area, although not in the news recently since their leader snuffed it last January."

"Snuffed it? Natural causes or some kind of gang warfare?" Angie asked.

"He met a grisly end at the hands of a rival gang. I have it in my mind that the case is still open. I'll need to check into that side of things," Colin said.

"Did your contact say anything else, Colin?"

He nodded. "Yep, along with the name, he also told me that they've recently put the word out on the street for new recruits."

Angie contemplated his answer for a second or two. "Interesting. Do you think the new leader is recruiting members so that a revenge attack can be carried out?"

"I wouldn't put it past him. Not sure how these burglaries are fitting into things, mind."

Scott grunted. "I'd take a punt the gang are using these attacks as some kind of warning. They want to show the rival gangs in the area that they're still as dominant as ever, even though their leader has departed. Just thinking out loud, guys."

"And it's a good thought, Scott," Colin agreed. "I think we need to find out everything we can about these gang members, especially the newer ones."

"Would it be worth putting a surveillance team out on the streets?" Tommy asked.

Angie nodded, a slow thoughtful nod. She enjoyed watching her team jump into action with their thought process. "We might have something here. Any volunteers for surveillance? Ideally, faces that aren't known on the streets." She scanned the room. The team members' background information ran through her mind. "Frank and Jill, how do you both feel about teaming up for a surveillance operation?"

Jill shrugged and nodded. "Why not? It makes sense for a woman to be out there. Less obvious to any onlookers, I suspect."

Angie turned to face a puzzled Frank. "Something wrong, Frank?"

"Not really. I suppose I've never really thought about getting involved in surveillance antics before."

Angie suppressed a laugh at his choice of words. *Surveillance antics!* "Well, I really don't want any division in this team. I know we all have our own talents and weaknesses, but I think the more we're all willing to push ourselves and deal with the different angles of policing we need to cover, the more it will work in our favour in a big way. What do you say, Frank? Are you willing to give it a shot?"

"If you put it that way, then who am I to argue, boss? As long as Jill doesn't start any funny business in the car, then we should get on like the proverbial house on fire."

Jill laughed. "Wishful thinking on your part, sonny. I have a rebuttal to that: as long as Frank has had a shower today, I'm willing to give it a try."

Angie clapped her hands together. "Excellent news. I do love it when team members are keen to push the boundaries at work. Let's see if we can obtain as much info about this Streetlife as possible before you set off."

"Will it mean an overnight surveillance?" Frank asked hesitantly.

"Well, seeing that all the murders and attacks have taken place during the daylight hours, I'm not sure that'll be necessary, Frank. Would you have a problem with the task if it was overnight? It might be something we need to consider in the future, either on this assignment or another one that crops up."

He looked sheepish. "Just asking, boss. I have a date planned for this evening, that's all. Forget I asked."

Angie smiled. "It's forgotten already. The quicker we get to work now, the sooner you and Jill can get on with the surveillance, okay?"

The team hit their keyboards, and soon, the information on the gang came flooding in. When it was all presented to Angie, she sat at her desk quietly for ten minutes to consume the details and slot it into some semblance of order.

"Wow, that's some rap sheet. Does anyone know of the gang personally?"

The team remained silent.

"Let's see. Hmm... this is interesting. The current leader has only been in charge for a few months by the looks of things, since his predecessor was gunned down by a rival gang. Does anyone have more intimate knowledge of this gang or the leader's murder?" Angie scanned the team. "Colin?"

He tapped his forehead. "I know of the gang, but just in passing. I've never really had any form of dealings with them myself."

Angie nodded. "Never mind." She smiled, understanding it was impossible to keep abreast of every crime in London.

"I'll do some more digging if you like, boss."

"You do that, Colin. Looking down the list of suspected crimes, only a few of these have actually come to court, heaven knows why. However, the cases we're dealing with now don't really seem to be something usually associated with the gang. Any ideas about that?"

Colin shrugged. "New gang leaders usually like to change things. They have bright ideas of their own that they're frequently champing at the bit to implement."

"Or maybe it's a smokescreen meant to point the finger at their rival gang? Is this gang toying with us?"

"I agree with you, boss," Colin chimed in.

"Did your contact give any reason why he thought Streetlife was behind the murders?"

"He just said they were recruiting."

Angie placed her hand around her chin. "It all sounds too convenient to me. Has your snitch ever let you down before, Colin?"

"No, I can't say he has. Maybe the new leader isn't all he's cracked up to be. Perhaps he's screwed up from day one, has no idea what it takes to lead a gang, thought it would be a breeze, but in reality…"

"You could be on to something. Find out everything you can about the new gang leader. I'd like to get on with the surveillance right away, all the same. Frank, Jill, are you both ready to set off? We'll keep you up to date with what information comes to light."

Jill grabbed her coat and was out the door before Angie had finished her sentence. Frank, on the other hand, stood up and neatly pushed his chair under his desk before he pulled on his jacket and followed his new colleague out the door. If Angie had any doubts about a team member, it was with Frank. She hoped he was just going through a settling-down phase, but she planned on keeping an eye on his demeanour in the coming few days. If it didn't change, she would need to take him to one side to ask him what his problem was.

While the rest of the team got on with their research, Angie decided to visit the hospital, which was about twenty minutes from the station, to check on Maxine in person. The duty doctor spared her five minutes in his busy schedule to tell her there was no change in Maxine's condition. All the medical staff could do was wait and let her body heal itself. Because of the differences in the previous two cases, Angie decided to reach out to Maxine's next of kin to see if they could shed any light on the attack. The doctor had said that Maxine's mother was waiting in the nearby family waiting room. Angie entered the room and walked up to the woman who had her head buried in her hands.

"Hello, Mrs. Dyer?"

"Yes. Who are you?" the woman demanded brusquely.

"Sorry, I'm Detective Inspector Angie North of the Organised Crime Team. I came over to see if there was any news on your daughter. I'm looking into the attack."

"Have you found the person responsible for her being here? If only Kevin had been at home."

"Is Kevin Maxine's husband?"

"No, her boyfriend. Have you found the person yet?" Mrs. Dyer repeated.

Angie sighed. "No, not yet. I wondered if you can give me a little background information on your daughter."

"Such as? Are you insinuating that she brought this attack on herself?"

"Not in the slightest. I suppose in a roundabout way what I'm asking is if your daughter has any enemies? Such as an ex-boyfriend who possibly found the break-up hard to deal with?"

"Definitely not, Inspector! My daughter is not generally in the habit of making enemies. She's always treated people with kindness and respect, how she would like people to treat her. It's what I instilled in my children during their upbringing. That's why I'm flabbergasted someone would do this to her. My God, I could even end up losing her, for what? Because someone wanted a few of her possessions? What is the world coming to? Had the sick, lowlife just asked for whatever it was they wanted, she would have handed everything over willingly—she's that type of girl. Material things don't really mean anything to her. Family means the world to her, nothing else."

"Thank you for that, Mrs. Dyer. It'll certainly help us with our enquiries. Have the doctors given you any idea on how long your daughter will be unconscious?" She kicked herself for forgetting to ask the doctor moments earlier.

"How long is a piece of string, Inspector? They can't possibly know. There's every chance my baby has suffered some form of brain damage; of course the doctors won't be sure of that until she wakes up."

"I'm so sorry to hear that, Mrs. Dyer. I've asked the hospital to ring me when she regains consciousness. I hope that's okay?"

"So you can start bombarding her with questions she most likely will struggle to answer? Do you really think she's going to be able to name her attacker?"

"No, but I'll still need to get some form of statement from your daughter. Of course, I will treat her injuries sympathetically."

"Sympathetically? What's the matter with going out on the street and carrying out some legwork investigation for a change? Isn't that what your lot tend to avoid nowadays?"

Angie winced when the angry woman turned her back. She drove back to the station with Mrs. Dyer's scathing parting dig ringing in her ears. Years of government cutbacks to the Met meant that the woman's damning statement was right, up to a point. The general public's trust was waning due to these cutbacks too, and Angie feared it would be a long time before the force recovered the people's trust. She and her team had a job to do to restore the public's faith.

When she reached the office, feeling a little deflated, she sat down at her desk to prepare her speech for the conference due to take place after lunch. With little to go on, except a gang name from a source who might have fed them misinformation, her hopes lay with the chance that someone would come forward with a gem of a clue.

CHAPTER SEVEN

The journalists shuffled in their chairs, waiting patiently for the conference to begin. Although Angie was assigned to be the spokesperson in charge of making the announcement to the world's media, she had invited DCI Channing to attend with her, if only to offer moral support. He had beamed when she'd turned up at his office half an hour before to make the request, and he'd assured her that he wouldn't intervene unless she specifically instructed him to. And now they sat together, ready for action.

Angie took a final sip from her glass of water as a hush descended over the crowd. "I'd like to thank you all for attending this conference today. Our main intention is to highlight three ongoing cases and to ask for the public's help in bringing justice to the victims. Two of the cases are from incidents which took place a few months ago, in which both victims lost their life. These are being treated as murder enquiries. The third victim is currently unconscious in hospital.

"All three victims were attacked in their own homes. From the witness statements we've gathered so far, we believe the attacker gained access to the women's homes under the guise of being a courier of some description. What we're asking is, has anyone out there had any experience of this type of thing happening in their area? Or has anyone had the misfortune of finding themselves in a similar situation in the South London area and haven't reported the crime to the police? Maybe a neighbour has mentioned something, either about themselves or someone they know. Please, the more information we can gather about these crimes, the quicker we'll be able to apprehend and arrest the criminals. May I remind you that they have killed two young women already?"

Angie then went into detail about where the crimes took place, named the dead victims, and gave a vague description of how the crimes occurred, including that they took place in broad daylight. That fact alone placed the journalists in a spin. Murmurs rippled through the crowd, mainly coming from the female members. Once Angie had finished, the questions came thick and fast, as she'd suspected they would.

"Inspector, why do you think the suspects have escaped capture for so long?" a young, female blonde reporter asked.

"The first two cases, while they were both perplexing, weren't dealt with appropriately." Angie cast an awkward glance at DCI Channing, who nodded for her to continue. "The Organised Crime Team were only given the cases yesterday, but already, we've uncovered more details about the crimes than the original investigating officers had in the weeks they dealt with them."

"Are you some sort of clean-up team?" a middle-aged male reporter sporting a greying beard asked.

Angie smiled and tilted her head from side to side. "Well, I wouldn't necessarily call us a clean-up team as such. Sometimes, in cases like this, it's often difficult to see what's right in front of you."

The reporter snorted. "Really, Inspector? Are you saying in a roundabout way that you think the cases were investigated by morons?"

Angie narrowed her gaze. "As I've already stated, these cases have come to our attention because they weren't dealt with appropriately. With the latest attack being very similar to the first two cases, I felt it was important to make this announcement and plea for information immediately."

"So, are you saying the investigating officers on the first two cases neglected to do that?" the male reporter asked, again going for the jugular.

Angie looked him in the eye and held his gaze for a moment or two. "If it's all the same to you, I really don't want this meeting to be about apportioning blame. Our aim should be to rid the streets of these vile criminals, and quickly. We can only do that if people—by that, I mean other criminals out there or members of the public—are willing to confide in us. I want to assure everyone listening, my team will do their utmost to rectify any wrongs relating to the first two cases. We're determined to bring these cases to a swift conclusion, but again, we need *your* help to obtain our objective."

"You're in charge of the Organised Crime Team—does that hint at these crimes being thought of as more dangerous than any other ongoing crimes?" The male reporter grinned broadly.

You're sharp, mate. Maybe too sharp for your own good. Angie looked at DCI Channing. "Actually, I'm not in charge of the team. That's DCI Channing's responsibility. However, our team is tackling this case because two murders have been committed. We're a tough team and will do what's necessary to arrest the culprits."

"Meaning what, Inspector?"

She smiled and hitched up her right shoulder. "As I said, we'll do whatever we deem necessary to rid the streets of such evil. We *have* to." Angie's gaze drifted around the crowd in front of her. "Any more questions?"

"Just one, Inspector, if I may?" the bearded reporter raised his hand.

"And that is?" Angie asked, her smile never wavering.

"You mentioned a vehicle had been seen at the locations, yet you haven't supplied us with a registration number. That seems a little odd to me."

"There's a reason for that, one that I'm not willing to address at this moment in time. All I can give you is that a black four-by-four was used for the crimes."

The reporter narrowed his eyes.

Angie decided to draw the session to a close before he had the chance to ask anything else. "Thank you for your attendance today. My team are ready and waiting for your calls if you feel you can supply us with further information about any of the cases."

DCI Channing stood, and Angie followed him out of the room. Once they were in the hallway, Angie threw her back against the wall and let out a huge sigh. "I hadn't expected that kind of grilling. Do you think it was too soon to call a press conference?"

"No, I don't. There's always some reporter willing to take the opportunity to make a name for themselves. I thought you handled him admirably. I doubt if I'd have shown him the amount of patience you did."

"Thanks, sir. That means a lot. Right, I suppose we better prepare ourselves for the onslaught of calls we're expecting."

"You really think there will be that many?" the chief asked as they ascended the stairs to their respective offices.

"I live in hope. The first thing I need to do is contact the surveillance team, see if they have anything to report."

"Let me know if you hear or need anything." He tapped her shoulder. "You did a great job back there. Continue with your good work."

Buoyed by his open show of appreciation for a job well done, she walked back into the team's office wearing a large grin.

"Good conference, I take it?" Tommy asked as soon as Angie stepped through the door.

"So-so. Anyone heard from Jill and Frank yet?"

Tommy shook his head. "No, I'd say it was too soon for that. Do you think we'll get much from the conference?"

"It's hard to say, Tommy. Let's be prepared for every eventuality, eh?"

* * *

The TV drew Dev's attention. A picture in the background showed a street on their patch. He upped the volume and called Duke. "You wanna watch this, man?"

Duke threw himself into the leather sofa. "What am I watching?"

"Seems like some kind of cop media session to me. Look in the background. That's Harris Court. Maybe we should check it out, see what's going on in our patch?"

"Keep it shut then." Duke upped the volume on the remote again. Once he heard the victims' names mentioned, he turned, wide-eyed, to look at Dev. "Did I hear right?"

Dev seemed puzzled. "What are you thinking?"

"Get the lists. Go back a few months."

Dev pushed himself out of the low sofa and marched over to his control centre in the corner of the room where his computer was stored, along with all the paperwork to do with the scam they were running. After locating his notebook in which he'd noted down what names the teams had successfully contacted and robbed, he returned to the sofa and handed it to Duke. "It don't look good, man."

Duke snatched the book out of his hand and flicked through the pages. He jabbed one specific name with his finger. "What the fuck? You remember that haul, don't ya? Tyler and Malc turned up here the next day with a pillowcase full of gear. That cop has just shown pictures of some of that jewellery. We got shot of it, didn't we?"

Dev nodded. "Shit! Yeah, but this could still turn ugly on us, man. Wasn't that their first job?"

"Yeah. Fuck, they killed her. They told us no one was home." He launched himself out of the chair faster than an Exocet missile and stormed across the room. When he reached the window, he leaned his temple against the cold glass and started banging his head rhythmically, each smack harder than the last. He scanned the car park below and noticed Tyler's car. He spun around. "Jesus! They're on their way up here. I ain't got a clue how to handle this, man. This wasn't part of the scam. Shit! How long is it gonna be before the cops come knocking on my door, eh?"

"You've gotta get rid of him—them. Malc is as much a part of this as Tyler is. It's the quiet ones you have to watch."

Duke paced the floor, his blood racing through his veins, unsure what to do next. *Should I pounce on the men the second they step through the door and bash the truth out of them? Or bite my tongue and mull things over?* The men were in a deep well of shit. "I need to think about this. Act natural when they come up. Don't let on about what we've just seen. Turn the TV off in case it comes on again while they're here. We'll get rid of them ASAP and then decide what we're gonna do about this mess."

Dev threw his arms out to the side. "I don't know if I can act like nothing has happened, Duke. These guys are friggin' nuts! How do we know they're not planning on bumping us off next?"

"Calm down. They know I've got more than one nine-piece in the flat. They wouldn't try anything here. Just keep alert when they're around for now. Get that fuckin' scared look off your face, or they'll cotton on something is going down."

Dev picked up the notebook and went back to his desk. "I've got the boys' routes planned out this morning. You want me to stick with them or what?"

"Might as well. Shit! I wish we'd friggin' known about this earlier."

"We could always put them off for twenty-four hours, man."

"I'm not sure, Dev. They know you're efficient and that we need to keep the money coming in regularly. It might make them suspicious. Why the fuck did we take these guys on?" There was a knock on the door. Duke motioned with his head for Dev to let the men in. "Act natural, remember?"

When Tyler and Malc walked into the room, they were empty-handed for a change. They fist-bumped Dev and crossed the room to do the same to Duke. "How's it hanging?" Tyler asked, chewing gum.

"Pretty good, man. We've got nothing for you today. How did it go yesterday?"

Tyler shrugged. "Nothing. I was hoping that today would be better. How come the action has dried up all of a sudden?"

"We've been a bit distracted with other business. Nothing to concern you. Things need sorting, dealing with immediately, that kinda thing. If you've got other work you can find for the next day or two, you should defo get on with that."

"Hey, I thought we were part of this gang. Let's help you out," Tyler replied swiftly.

Duke turned his back on the man and looked out the window again while he trawled his mind for another excuse to get rid of them. "Nah, some things just need mine and Dev's brainpower to deal with. Take some time off. You've earned it, man. You're the best we got." He hoped his jovial response sounded convincing.

Tyler punched his mate's shoulder and walked back to the door. "Come on, Malc. I get the impression our services ain't needed around here no more."

Duke spun round to face him. "I never said that, man. We got stuff to sort out. Give us twenty-four hours, right?"

"Whatever. You've got my number; give me a shout." Tyler and Malc left the flat and slammed the door shut behind them.

Dev blew out the breath he'd been holding in and collapsed against the back of his chair. "Jesus, that was close."

Duke shot him a warning glance to keep his mouth shut. "Give it five." He stared out of the window until he spotted the men, then he sighed heavily too. "Fuck, he's a suspicious shit, ain't he?"

"We've gotta think up something quick, Duke. I'm sensing that they ain't gonna be that easy to get rid of. You've just gotta forget about the hauls they've brought in and think of the murders they've committed. I want no part of that side of things."

Duke turned to face his second in command. "Man, toughen up, that is if you wanna stick with Streetlife. Yeah, I'm gonna do all I can to get rid of Tyler and Malc, but when they go, there's gonna be others who come along and step out of line. We're meant to own these fuckin' streets, for fuck's sake. Death and murder is a given. Take Leroy, for instance. When he was murdered, I didn't hear you shouting you wanted out then, did I?"

Dev's head dropped, and his chin hit his chest. "I know! But, Duke, this is a different ball game. I just can't deal with innocent women being killed. Hey…" He glanced up to look Duke in the eye, then continued, "You're forgetting one major thing, man."

"Am I? What's that?"

"The copper said there's a woman in hospital. Shit, man, if she wakes up and identifies Tyler and Malc, then that's it. Game over."

"Damn, I never thought of that. What do ya think we should do about the girl?"

Dev shook his head. "Ain't got a clue. Where's the doubt sprung from, man?"

"My head's tied up in knots. I'm no Leroy. Being the leader is new, and this shit is hard. I'm fucked—we all are—whatever I decide to do. That includes you!"

"Easy, man, I hear you. But you've gotta think up a way of getting rid of Tyler and Malc, before they drag us into all this crap."

CHAPTER EIGHT

The phones rang consistently throughout the afternoon, and Angie's team dealt with the calls, mostly hoaxes, proficiently. Around four thirty, Jill and Frank returned to the station. Jill seemed bright and in a buoyant mood, while Frank looked as if someone had put a dent in the side of his car.

Angie hung up the phone from a caller who swore blind he'd seen the man leaving Maxine Dyer's house, only to laugh and slam the phone down. "Effing moron!" she grumbled. She looked up at Jill. "I hope your exploits have harvested more than we've managed around here."

Jill pulled up the nearest chair and sank into it while Frank folded his arms and leaned against the nearby desk. "Well, we located the gang leader's flat and watched the comings and goings of the area for a few hours. At first, we didn't see anything to get excited about until two men turned up in a black four-by-four."

Her interest mounted, Angie sat forward in her chair. "Really? Okay, there's no point asking if you got the registration number or not, because we reckon they keep changing them, but did you get a good look at the men?"

"Yep, they didn't try to hide their identity at all. Why would they? They had no reason to do that on their own patch. I'm going to look through the database, see if I can put a name to the faces. Neither of us recognised them anyway."

"That's a shame. So they arrived at the location, then what?"

Jill shrugged. "They walked inside the block of flats and surprisingly returned to the car five to ten minutes later."

Angie frowned. "Do you think they turned up to report in? To get their orders for the day?"

"It's hard to tell. They appeared to be pretty pissed off about things when they came out, didn't they, Frank?" Jill asked, obviously trying to include her partner in the conversation.

"Yeah, they were none too pleased," he agreed, hitching up his shoulder.

"What if they saw the conference?" Angie asked.

"I suppose it was around the same time it was due to go on air," Jill said, looking thoughtful.

"Right, Jill, we've got an hour or so before we knock off for the day. Can you search the database for these guys? The sooner we can identify them, the quicker we can pull them in for a roasting."

"I'll get on it now." Jill rushed over to her desk and brought her computer screen to life before she sat down.

"Frank, can you help Tommy go through the list of callers, start ringing some of these people back? I need to keep on top of these calls as and when they come in; otherwise, we're going to be snowed under in no time." Frank nodded and walked over to Tommy, who handed him a small pile of notes.

Angie picked up the phone and rang the next number on her list, a lady by the name of Gertrude Collins. "Hello. Mrs. Collins?"

"Yes. Who's this?" the woman replied.

"This is DI Angie North. You rang New Scotland Yard earlier today with regard to a crime committed in your area. Is that right?"

"Yes, that's right. I saw that nice young officer on the TV at lunchtime asking for people to ring in and help with her enquiries."

"I appreciate that, Mrs. Collins. I'm the officer you saw on the screen. What can you tell us about the crime?"

"Pretty thing you are. My hair used to be your colour when I was younger. Men always found it a struggle dealing with my fiery temper. How about you, dear? Do you get grief for flying off the handle at a moment's notice?"

Angie covered the mouthpiece of the phone, laughed then cleared her throat before she responded, "Well, I've learned over the years that's what people expect of me, so I've tried my hardest to tone down my temper. About the crime, Mrs. Collins? Would you mind going over what you saw again?"

"What? Over the phone? Don't your lot do house calls any more?"

"Would you rather I came out to take a statement from you?"

"No. Don't waste your time, dear. I can't say I really saw much anyway. I thought it best to ring and tell you what I did see. Hopefully it'll help you build a picture of the events of what happened that day."

"If you don't mind me saying, Mrs. Collins, you sound like you worked on the force."

"Not I, dear, but my dearly departed husband. He retired one week and was dead the next. I think he just gave up. Never really wanted to retire. He was pressured into it, to make way for a group of youngsters the Met wanted to recruit. I bet half of them never made it through the training course."

Angie nodded. "I suspect you're probably right. Going back to the incident, if I may? What exactly did you see?"

"That car you described, it pulled up, and a man exited the vehicle. Then the phone rang. It was the hospital wanting me to complete some kind of survey after my short stay in Saint Thomas's. By the time I'd finished the call, the car had gone."

"The man. Would you be able to identify him again?"

"In a line-up?"

"Yes."

"I'm not sure, dear. It all happened so quickly. I doubt my observation skills are up to scratch with my bad eyesight. Well, it's not now as I've recently had a cataract operation—that's why I was in hospital."

"I see. Never mind. I suppose it's back to the drawing board for us then. Take care, Mrs. Collins. Thank you for contacting us."

"Not at all. I know right from wrong, dear, and you mark my words: I knew from the moment I laid eyes on that man that he was up to no good. May I ask how Maxine is?"

"All I can tell you is she's in a coma. We're hoping she'll wake up soon and be able to fill in the blanks for us."

"I'll say a little prayer for her throughout the day, dear. Sorry I couldn't be more help. Good luck with your investigation, and you have my permission to drop your guard on that temper of yours when you catch up with the bastard who did this. In fact, give him a kick in the goolies from me."

"I'll be sure to do that, Gertrude. Take care now." Angie hung up and laughed loudly. "Guys, I've been given the authority to kick the offender in the nuts when we catch up with him."

The rest of the team chuckled, splitting the tension in the office.

"How are you doing, Tommy?"

The young detective shook his head. "Not good. Nothing at all really." His gaze drifted over to the far wall.

"Okay, what are you thinking?" Angie asked.

"I think it would be worth getting someone on the inside."

"Maybe we could go down that route eventually. I think it might be too soon for that now, Tommy. Let's hang back until Maxine comes round, eh?"

"Ah, but it could be too late by then. What if these guys kill someone else in the meantime?"

"It's the chance we have to take. To send a member of the team in undercover when we have very little to go on would be suicidal, wouldn't it?"

Tommy shrugged. "Maybe you're right about that."

"Let's do some more digging and try and find out how ruthless this gang and its members can be before we insert someone, okay?"

"Agreed."

The team continued to field the calls and search their computer databases for the next hour or so before Angie clapped her hands to gain their attention. "Okay, guys, we've done our best for the day. Let's go home, grab some rest, and start again tomorrow."

Half an hour later, Angie walked into the kitchen of her home and found her son at the table, bent over his homework. He had his iPhone beside him and his headphones in. She tapped him on the shoulder, and the shock almost propelled him upstairs via the kitchen ceiling.

"Crap, Mum!"

"Language, Luke." She gave him one of her chastising looks.

"That's not swearing. Just be thankful I didn't drop an f-bomb for you scaring the crap out of me like that."

"Maybe that's something you need to be aware of in the future, love."

"What? You mean I need to have eyes in the back of my head just in case you creep up on me?"

Angie snorted. "That's not what I meant, and you know it. Has Dad rung?"

"Would that be my dad or yours?"

Angie sucked on the inside of her mouth to prevent herself from slapping him down. Luke had become problematic in the last few months, eager to start an argument at every given moment. She and Warren had chatted regularly about how to combat his attitude and were still searching for the answer. Angie knew she was easier on her son because he was their only child. He was a genius in her book, and his talent needed to be nurtured, not restricted. In spite of his willingness to start an argument, he hadn't shown any signs of neglecting his schoolwork, and to her, that was a blessing.

"You know your grandfather is struggling to get out of bed at the moment. Why the sarcasm, Luke? Is there something you want to have a chat about?" Angie sat down beside him and placed her hand over his.

He snatched his hand away and stared at his homework.

Angie was at a loss for what to do next: carry on probing or let things lie? She sighed and leaned back in her chair. "When you're ready to talk, you know where I am."

"I don't need to talk. I'm doing my homework, Mum. Jeez, you have a go at me when I don't have my head in my books, and when I do, you're still on my case. I can't win." He gathered his books, scraped his chair over the tiled floor, and stormed out of the room.

Her eyes filled up with tears of frustration. Through her job, she came into contact with too many mothers who didn't have an open relationship with their child. She'd always considered Luke to be different from boys of his age—she hadn't expected him to turn that on its head and become a rebellious teenager. The front door banged, shaking her from her thoughts. Warren walked into the kitchen wearing a beaming smile, which slipped when he met her gaze. She wiped away her tears with the back of her hand and stood up. They met halfway and hugged each other. Even after so many years together, they knew when to be silent and just cling to one another for support.

Angie patted his back, pushed out of his arms, and crossed the room to fill the kettle. "How was your day?"

"Good, compared to yours, judging by your appearance. Want to talk about it?"

"Later. Let's get dinner on the go first. Why was your day so good?"

Warren took the meat joint out of the fridge and began washing it under the tap. "All my doubts about Haden's abilities proved to be unfounded. I got a call from the accountants we laid on the function for, and they were delighted by how it all went. They've given us some firm bookings for every month leading up to Christmas."

Angie squealed. "Darling, that's wonderful news. The best thing about this is that it'll give you more freedom, right?"

"That's the plan. Couldn't have come at a worse time for you, though, having just accepted your new promotion."

"We'll get around that. I'll just delegate more."

Warren's eyebrow rose, and he tilted his head. "Really? Who are you trying to kid?"

Angie placed a hand over her face and dipped her head. "I thought if I said it out loud there'd be more chance of it actually coming true."

Her husband tutted and placed the beef in the roasting tin. "You keep telling yourself that, love. How's the case going? Was that why you were upset?"

"No. The *cases* are progressing slowly. The DCI and I held a press conference today, and we were inundated with calls, most of which were time-wasters. You know how it is with these things. Something interesting has come to our attention, though—we believe the cases to be gang related. Our idea still needs verification, but that's what it looks like we're dealing with."

"Yowzer! Now that's frightening. So a gang is going around killing women in their own homes? For what reason? Just to burgle them, or are we looking at something more sinister than that here?"

"Like I say, that's as much as we have for now. We're still sifting through the calls we received, but I did put a team out on surveillance today. They didn't really get any clear indication that the two men they spotted were up to anything, but their behaviour was a little off."

"Surveillance already? So you must be pretty sure about your facts to organise that so soon in your case. Am I right?"

"Spot on. Our original information came from one of the team's informants on the street. I took a chance that the info was good and put a plan into action. I suspect we'll need more than a few hours surveillance under our belts to bring these guys down, though."

"It's a start. That's the main thing. So why were you so down when I came home?"

"Self-pity! Oh, I don't know. I'm just at a loss what to do about Luke. Do you think there's something going on with him that we're unaware of?"

"Undoubtedly, it's called hormones. Think back to when you were a teenager. How did you react when you spoke to your parents?"

"Always with respect. You know Dad—he wouldn't have stood for any nonsense. Although Darren felt the brunt of his anger a few times, or rather his ears did."

"Ah, okay, yes. I can imagine John doing that when your brother was cheeky. You and Darren have both turned out well, haven't you?"

Angie pointed her finger and wagged it from side to side. "No. Don't even go there, buster. I refuse to go down that route. Beating the crap out of him isn't the answer, Warren."

"I know it's not. I'm just saying that if Luke is becoming difficult, then it's better if we stamp it out now rather than have to deal with the consequences later."

"Okay, I'm listening! What are you suggesting?"

"We go away for the weekend—the three of us, for a bonding session."

Angie let out a relieved sigh. *I should have known Warren better than that.* "I think it's a great idea, except…"

"Except what?"

"Well, I've just taken on a new case, and it depends what crops up over the next few days as to whether I can afford to take the weekend off or not."

Warren rolled his eyes up to the ceiling. "I get it. Maybe it would be better if we planned a weekend away rather than just plump for the first weekend that comes up."

"Now you're talking."

"We'll discuss it and have a look on the net for availability after dinner, eh?" Warren planted a kiss on her lips, and together, they finished preparing the meal.

After dinner, Angie fired up the laptop, then she and Warren picked out a quaint little retreat on a holiday cottage website and booked it for the following month. Angie drifted off to sleep hoping they had made the right decision about taking Luke with them. Would a teenage boy be thrilled at the prospect of tagging along with his parents on a weekend away?

CHAPTER NINE

Angie was the first member of the team to arrive at work. She grabbed a coffee and sat at her desk. While sorting through the messages that had come the team's way since the conference, she placed aside one in particular that captured her interest. She was deep in thought, her mind running faster than an express train, when Tommy breezed into the room.

"Morning, boss. Nice day."

Angie smiled at him. *Ah, the enthusiasm of youth!* "Morning, Tommy. Grab a coffee and join me."

His brow furrowed, he collected a coffee, pulled up a chair next to her, and took the sheet of paper from her outstretched hand. "Relating to our cases, I take it?"

"Tell me what you think of that one?"

He studied the slip of paper carefully and set it aside. "I can see the similarity; however, it's the glaring difference screaming out at me. Should we be cautious about linking this to our ongoing cases?"

Angie was proud he'd regarded the information in exactly the same way she had. "I agree. Nevertheless, something is telling me we would be foolish to ignore the information. Would you care to accompany me on a home visit, Tommy?"

"You don't have to ask twice. Ready when you are."

The door opened, and the rest of the team filtered in one by one. She greeted them all as they settled down at their desks and began their working day. Angie was confident the rest of the team were busy following up other leads, and so within half an hour, she and Tommy were en route to speak to a woman whose note had interested Angie. The victim, a Janet Lawrence, was at home when they arrived.

"Miss Lawrence? I'm Detective Inspector Angela North, and this is my partner, Detective Sergeant Tommy O'Brien." They each flashed their warrant card for her to study carefully.

The young woman nodded and nervously opened the front door wider to allow the detectives access into her home. "Please, come in."

They followed the woman into the first room off the hallway. Angie noticed how much the woman's hands shook as she recounted her story.

"So, you weren't actually at home when the robbery took place?" Angie asked.

"No. But as soon as I heard you on the TV yesterday I had a gut feeling it could be related, so thought I'd get in touch, just in case."

"What gave you that idea exactly, Miss Lawrence?"

"You said the criminals were possibly pretending to be couriers of sorts. Well, I remember receiving a call from a courier firm the day before the burglary. They wanted to know when I would be at home so they could deliver a parcel to me."

"I see. Did you ever receive the parcel in question?"

She shook her head, and her mouth turned down at the sides. "No. Never. And it didn't occur to me to mention it when I reported the crime. You see, it all happened very quickly. The so-called courier rang me in the morning and explained they wanted to rearrange a delivery. I said I'd be home all that day if it was convenient for them. I also told them that the next day wouldn't be any good as I'd be back at work."

"So they knew your home would be empty?"

"Yes, stupid of me really to give that kind of information over the phone. I've seen all kinds of scams, people posting warnings on Facebook and spam e-mails. But I honestly thought it was a legitimate delivery company. The connection only crossed my mind when I saw your appeal on TV. I haven't stopped trembling since I watched it. The thought that I could have been one of those women... well, it's just awful." She shuddered as her eyes moistened.

Angie sat next to the woman and covered her hand with her own. "Please, you mustn't think like that. Your case might not be connected to the ones we're investigating. It's really not worth putting yourself through hell thinking about it."

"What sort of world are we living in when people think nothing about breaking into your home? They seem keen to rob hard-working people of the simple belongings they've saved hard for and collected over the years."

"Is there anything else that you can tell us about the caller, Miss Lawrence? Something this person might have said? Or perhaps they had a distinctive accent?"

Janet sighed. "No, not that I can think of. I suppose he had a London accent. That's as much as I can tell you really. I'm sorry."

"Don't be. You're doing great. Do you have any form of security here? An alarm perhaps?" Angie asked.

"No, nothing."

"Can I suggest you get one, if you can afford it."

"I *can't*—afford it, I mean."

Tommy cleared his throat. "I know some people who just put one of those red boxes up above their front door. You know, it'll just give the impression that the house has an alarm fitted. Act as a minor deterrent at least.

Could you get a relative or friend to put one of those up for you perhaps?"

The woman's eyes lit up with relief. "Really? You think that works?"

Tommy smiled and nodded. "What harm can it do?"

"Then I'll see if my brother will do it for me, in between girlfriends," she joked, looking more at ease.

"Good. That's settled then. I take it you've had no other hassles since the robbery occurred?" Angie asked.

"No. Mind you, there was very little of value left for them to take if they returned."

"Your insurance covered your losses, hasn't it?"

"Sort of. You know what they're like. Sometimes, I think *they're* the criminals, not the burglars. They always seem to wriggle their way out of coughing up, at least they have in my case."

"I'm sorry to hear that, Miss Lawrence. Was there a clause in your contract, in the fine print?"

"No. They said it was clearly stated in the policy I took out that they wouldn't pay out on old for new, and most of my possessions were old. It's my fault—I should have kept the receipts for everything, but I didn't. It never dawned on me that I'd ever be targeted by a burglar. I know it's not the safest neighbourhood, but you just never think it's going to happen to you."

"I know it's difficult. Maybe the insurance company will have a bout of conscience and think twice when sending out your cheque."

Janet shook her head. "Nope, they've already paid out. Five hundred measly pounds they sent me. Tell me, what can you buy for that nowadays? I'll be changing my insurance next time it comes up for renewal."

"And who could blame you. That's appalling. I'm sorry. Get that box fitted ASAP, would be my advice," Angie warned with a smile.

The woman gasped. "Are you saying that you think the burglars will return? Is that what they do? Rob a house and return once the insurance company has paid out? Is that how these type of things work?"

Angie raised her hands in front of her as the woman bombarded her with questions. "It's not something we've encountered before. Sorry if I gave you that impression. I just meant having the box installed will give you peace of mind, if nothing else."

The woman seemed to calm down, and Angie nodded at Tommy. They both stood up to leave.

"Miss Lawrence, take my card, and if you think of anything else, don't hesitate to call me directly," Angie said.

They made their way outside, then the woman engaged the double bolt lock on the front door.

"God, she's shaken up, Angie. I hope we haven't made things worse when actually it's just a coincidence," Tommy said once they were in the car.

"I have a feeling this attack wasn't that. Perhaps someone new on the scene has upped their game, got greedy, and decided not to wait for the homeowners to leave the property."

"Ah, it's disgusting. We need to catch this son of a bitch—excuse my French—before he ruins another helpless woman's life."

"No need to apologise, Tommy. I feel exactly the same. Let's get back to the station and regroup with the rest of the team."

They returned to an upbeat atmosphere in the office. Colin bounced over to Angie, a wide grin spreading across his face.

"Well, this looks positive."

"You're going to like this, boss."

"Come on, Colin. Spit it out."

"A young lad was picked up by uniform about an hour ago. He was trying to offload items to a jeweller in Brixton. One of the items matches the ring taken from Heather Moriarty."

"The first victim who was murdered?" Tommy interjected.

"Yes, the very same. The jeweller saw your appeal and called 999. He pretended to be interested in the gear and was pondering what to buy with the intention of stalling the guy. The kid was still at the shop when the squad car turned up."

A fire ignited inside Angie. She'd been concerned a break in the case would pass them by, but she suddenly saw a twinkle of hope. "Has he been interviewed? What's his name?"

"Chris Strange. And no, as soon as I found out, I got DCI Channing involved. He said we'd take over and that no one was to question the boy until you returned to the station."

"Well done, Colin. Fab work. You should've called me. I would've returned sooner."

"I knew you wouldn't be long, so I used the time to delve into Strange's background."

Colin's smile returned, and Angie couldn't help but mirror his expression. It was obvious he was holding back another gold nugget of information.

"Strange has been in and out of foster care since he was five years old. He has a long rap sheet, nothing along the lines of the attacks pertaining to our crimes. However, the system threw up a link to Leroy Charles."

"The former gang leader of Streetlife? Ah, Jesus, folks," Tommy shouted and perched against his table.

"Colin, I could kiss you!" Angie said light-heartedly. "That is fantastic work. Is DCI Channing up to speed on your developments?"

"No, boss. But he said he wanted a word with you when you got back."

Angie relieved Colin of the printed reports. "Right, I'll quickly update the chief about Strange. As you've collated all this, Colin, do you want to sit in on the interview with me?"

Colin peered at Tommy. "Are you all right with that?"

"Of course, don't be daft." Tommy thumped Colin's shoulder. "You've done an excellent job so far. You've earned the right to interrogate the little shit."

Both men laughed, and Angie was delighted to see their camaraderie.

CHAPTER TEN

Angie sat opposite Chris Strange in Interview Room One, staring at him, while Colin voiced the obligatory information for the sake of the recording machine and the duty solicitor jotted notes on his legal pad. Angie studied the young man, barely out of his teens, cockiness oozing from every pore. Arms folded tightly across his chest, he was slouched casually in the chair, smirking as he stared back at her. But Angie looked deeper into his dark brown eyes that shone out against his pale skin. She could tell he'd encountered things in his young life that no twenty-year-old should have. Unwilling to hold her stare any longer, he let his eyes dart around the room, from the door to Colin, then the table. She could tell his feisty resolve was crumbling. Panic replaced the defiance in his eyes, and large beads of sweat trickled down his forehead and seeped into his dark eyebrows.

"Chris, let's not play games with each other," Angie finally said. "You were caught red-handed with stolen items in your possession. One such item was ripped from the finger of a dead woman."

"What?" the boy shouted, his eyes doubling in size.

"Heather Moriarty was murdered in her home at the beginning of the year—"

"Hey! I ain't murdered *no one*!"

"Her family have identified the ring. They've informed us that she never took it off, which means she would have been wearing it at the time she was killed."

"You can't prove nothing, lady. I ain't no murderer," Chris protested.

"So, I'm fascinated to know how that same stolen ring was found in your possession today, in the Brixton pawn shop where you were arrested."

His aggression rose. "I found it."

Silence filled the small grey interview room. Angie remained calm and simply smiled at Chris.

His eyes flicked around the room once again. "I'm telling ya—I *found* the damn ring!"

"If that's the case, then why didn't you hand it in to the police, Mr. Strange?"

He hesitated. "Because I needed the money."

"I did suggest we be straight with one another. So, forgive me if I'm not willing to play the banal cat-and-mouse game with you and believe your 'I found the ring' story. We know you have an association with the Streetlife gang, in particular with its previous leader, Leroy Charles."

Chris wiped the sweat from his forehead on the back of his hand. The level of perspiration had increased as soon as Angie mentioned the gang's title. She deliberately hadn't posed a question yet. She'd intended only to observe the boy's reaction.

He shifted in his seat and shook his head vehemently. "Nah. You've got the wrong person."

"Are you sure about that, Mr. Strange? You're currently sitting in the police station, under arrest for the possession of stolen goods. Stolen from a murder victim, no less."

"You can't pin anything on me. I told ya—I ain't murdered no one."

The desperation in his voice sounded real. "So why protect them? I don't see any of your gang members rallying round to help you, now that you've been caught,

Mr. Strange. But maybe... well, maybe I could help you get out of this fix."

"What'cha mean?" His brow furrowed.

Angie left her offer dangling in the air for a few moments. She was aware the boy held the answers required for them to catch the murderer, possibly the entire gang. She also knew she would need to tread carefully or he might clam up. "Listen, Chris," she said in a friendlier tone, hoping her soft voice would entice the boy rather than scare him off. "It's simple. You help me out, give me the information I need about the victim, and I'll repay the favour. I'll ensure the judge is lenient on you for a crime you're telling me you didn't commit."

"I ain't no grass, lady," Chris said, but his voice held less conviction than his words.

"Well, DS Bishop"—Angie turned to face Colin—"I think we can wrap this interview up and draw up the arrest papers."

"Sure thing, boss. If the kid doesn't want to help, we have no other option but to hold him responsible for the murder." Colin reached out to switch off the recorder.

"Wait!" Chris shouted. He glanced at his solicitor. "Help me?"

The duty solicitor shrugged. "This is a very serious crime, Mr. Strange. I think it would be wise if you told the officers what you know. Otherwise, I have no doubt they'll do what they say and hold you accountable."

Angie touched Colin's arm to prevent him from switching off the machine. He turned to face her, and she winked at him. "I think Mr. Strange is ready to talk now, DS Bishop."

Chris let out a heavy sigh and dropped his head onto his chest. "Well, I ain't so sure."

"What are you unsure about, Chris?" Angie smiled in an attempt to make the boy trust her.

"If I tell you what I know, I'll be dead the second I get outta here. You gotta promise me some kind of protection or something."

Angie smiled. "Chris, if you help me secure an arrest, you'll have all the protection you need from Streetlife. Trust me."

"Okay." He gulped loudly.

She recognised the strain he was under, how tough it was going to be for him to divulge all he knew. The gangs in Brixton were notorious, and it was difficult to get the locals to speak up, let alone someone on the inside. "How long have you been a member of the gang?"

The boy bowed his head and stared at the table for a few moments. When he looked up, his expression was solemn. "I'm not really a member." He shrugged.

"Chris, we don't have time for bullshit. We know your background. We need you to be totally honest with us. Take your time and tell us what you know, okay?" Angie prompted.

"It's true. I was never really initiated into Streetlife because I never stay in one area for too long. Although I guess Brixton has always been a base for me, I've been in and out of foster homes all over London. Honestly, I think Leroy felt sorry for me. He used to let me hang out with them when I was in the area. I just used to chill with them, have a smoke, and that kinda shit. I wasn't ever involved in their scams." He paused and chewed on his lip. "It was shit when Leroy got gunned down. Real sad. Then Duke took over."

"Who's Duke? What's his surname?" Angie asked.

Chris frowned. "I dunno, actually. I know you ain't gonna believe me, but I dunno any of their surnames. I just know Duke and Dev are the two main men running Streetlife. They're like best friends. It's hard now 'cause the rival gangs have one over on 'em, so they're trying to stay on top, to make sure Streetlife's rep is what's keeping everyone in line. They're doing all they can to keep bringing in the cash; you know how it is."

Angie didn't know how it was, but she didn't want to stop Chris while he was singing sweetly.

"Well, anyway," he continued as if he were reading a book, "Duke needed some more bodies in the gang, so he put the word out that he was recruiting. He and Dev thought up this new scam. They've got some mobile numbers of people in the local area. They call them saying they have a delivery to make and get their address. Then, when they know no one is in the house, they rob the joint. They asked me to get rid of a few things for them, get the most money I could for the items. I've kinda been busy with other stuff; that loot you found on me should've been gone ages ago. Look, this thing with the dead chicks was a shock to Duke. I don't think he knew. It was the new guys, innit."

"And do you know their names?"

"Tyler and Malc. I thought they seemed a bit off from the beginning, but it ain't my place to say anything. I'm lucky Duke has let me hang out with them still since Leroy died. He's even let me get involved with little things on the street. Shit! What am I going to do now?"

"Well, you're not going to prison for murder, Chris. I think that's what you need to focus on right now."

"Shit! You've tricked me into saying all this, lady. I can't believe it. I'm a dead man. If Duke doesn't get me, then that friggin' Tyler will."

Tears filled the boy's eyes, and Angie almost felt sorry for him. Many people who'd suffered in the past turned to gangs for solace and ended up committing crimes. Colin wrote something on a piece of paper and pushed it across the desk to Angie. She read it. Appreciating her colleague's quick thinking, she smiled at him.

"Chris, do any members of the gang have a tattoo on their neck?"

He looked up from the table and fumbled with his fingers. "Erm... yes. Tyler has a black panther on his neck. Bit shit if you ask me, just looks like a huge blob of ink. I had to ask him what it was. Couldn't make it out for myself. That pissed him off."

Inside, Angie beamed. She was eager to get out of the interview room, update her team, and apprehend the murdering scum. "For your protection, Chris, we'll keep you here at the station until we've arrested these men."

"What's gonna happen to me?"

Angie stood up. "We'll talk about that in due course."

Colin terminated the interview for the tape, and the pair left the room. Angie informed the desk sergeant of her decision to keep Chris Strange locked up in a cell for his own protection until further notice. She would maintain her promise and keep him safe.

"Boss, he sang like a canary. I can't quite believe it," Colin said as they briskly made their way back to the office.

"We were bloody lucky! We handled him just right. If we'd picked up one of the other gang members, I'm sure we'd still be sitting there with very few answers."

Angie was surprised to find Jill smiling while hanging up the telephone. "Boss, that was the hospital. Maxine Dyer just woke up, and she's lucid."

"This day is getting better by the minute!" Angie clicked her fingers. "Colin, stay here and update the team. I want checks carried out on all the names Chris gave us. Tommy, come with me. Let's get to the hospital, see if we can get some form of statement from Maxine. I'll bring you up to speed on the info Chris shared in the car."

CHAPTER ELEVEN

Duke stood on the corner of Electric Avenue. The hustle and bustle from the market street meant his presence went unnoticed. African beats pounded from the nearby record shop, the smells of Caribbean food filled his nostrils, and for a moment, he was transported back to his grandmother's kitchen. As a boy, he'd spent hours watching her cook. Times had been easier back then. Nowadays, he often felt as if he were drowning in a world he no longer knew how to control.

His thoughts turned to Leroy. He'd ruled the streets of Brixton and shown Duke the easy way to gain money and the respect of others. In those days, Duke had been capable of anything with Leroy on the scene for backup, but Duke had to admit, if only to himself, that without Leroy around, he was sometimes significantly out of his depth. He closed his eyes and imagined Leroy in his shoes, dealing with the dilemma that had been thrust upon him, and soon realised that his mentor would have dealt with the problem in an instant, extinguishing any threat that dared to cross his path. Duke pulled his shoulders back. He knew what he had to do.

A red Subaru with tinted windows pulled up alongside Duke. He jumped in and fist-bumped Dev. His friend handed him a joint. Duke lit it and watched the Rizla paper sizzle. He inhaled deeply then blew out a cloud of grey smoke. His head hit the headrest, and he took another long pull on the joint before passing it back to Dev.

"So, what have you found out?" he asked.

"That woman who survived Tyler's attack is conscious."

Duke sparked back to life and sat up. He stared at his friend. A feeling of dread passed over him. "How d'ya know that?"

"I got a bitch at the hospital," Dev replied. "She rang me five minutes ago while I was driving over here. She said Maxine Dyer was awake and wanted to talk to the police."

"Shit! This is not what we fucking need. If she can identify Tyler and Malc, the police'll be knocking on our door."

"I don't think they'll grass us up, man."

Duke contemplated his friend's words. "You're right, Dev! We need to keep them on our side, for now."

"What do you mean?"

"If they're part of our gang, and they get caught 'cause of this fuck-up, they ain't gonna dig a deeper grave by pulling us into it. For now, we have to be their mates, their partners, pretend we want to help them out. Then when they least expect it, we'll shut them up."

"That could work."

"There's already enough chat about this on the TV. The last thing we want is this woman describing Tyler and Malc and people connecting them to Streetlife. And us! We need to keep her clear of the police. Can this nurse get us onto the ward?"

"Doubt it, Duke! She said the woman's being guarded round the clock by the pigs. There's no way we'd get past them without being spotted."

"It's not us they're looking for. Even if she talks, she's going to describe two white guys and we definitely ain't white, bro."

Dev held his own black hand out in front of him and sniggered. "I suppose, but it's still a bit risky."

Duke rested his head back again and let his mind wander as he continued to share the joint with Dev. He wished he'd listened to his instincts when Tyler and Malc had first turned up at his flat. He knew they were too cocky to take orders, but the huge bag of loot had won him over. That was why he existed, why the gang existed: to obtain all the money they could get their hands on. In the end, his greed, or the grief over losing Leroy, had clouded his judgement. He realised he needed to be smarter, to buck up his ideas, and to stop wallowing in self-pity. Man up and play the game as Leroy would have done. He stared out the window, watched the women rush by with bags of spices and meat, while the laid-back men stood in the shop doorways, chatting and laughing the day away. This was *his* patch, and he wasn't about to roll over and let two crazy no-mark yobs trample on Streetlife's reputation. He sighed heavily.

"What you thinking, man?" Dev asked, his voice thick.

When Duke turned to face his friend, Dev's eyes were bloodshot and glassy. A mirror image of his own, he imagined.

"I'm gonna take care of my shit. I ain't about to let no psycho losers shop me to the cops. We'll play it cool for now, even welcome them back into the fold. Make them feel part of the team. And then, when the time is right, I'll know when that is, we'll deal with them. But I don't want them on any of our jobs."

"Cool, man. I'm down with that."

"But I still wanna see that woman in the hospital."

"Duke!"

"Chill, man. I ain't gonna hurt no one. I just wanna see what she knows."

"Okay, I'll talk to my bitch, see what she can arrange."

"Good. Have you spoken to Chris recently?"

Dev shrugged. "Nah, ain't seen him for a few days."

"But he got rid of the loot from Tyler and Malc's raid, right?"

"He said he did. He'll be around to see us soon enough. He owes us money from the sales that he ain't stumped up yet."

"Right, we'll use him on the next haul then."

"You sure he's up to that? He seems a bit immature, Duke."

"He might be a prat, but Leroy trusted him—that means we should too. We'll just make sure he has a decent partner with him on the job."

"Yeah, man, but you do realise we'll have to recruit a few more heads if we're going to ditch the two psychos."

Duke snorted. "Real talk, we can't have a pair of crazy men caught up with Streetlife, man." The effects of the drugs took hold; they laughed so hard the car shook from side to side. "We'll sort someone out for Chris. For now, let's have some fun. Fuck it! Call that nurse bitch now."

CHAPTER TWELVE

Angie and Tommy waited in the hospital's family room as the nurse had instructed. Angie paced, impatiently waiting for the doctor to arrive, her desperation to question Maxine Dyer intensifying with every step she took. She feared the longer the woman spoke to her family, the more likely the prominent details she had of her attacker would fade. The door finally opened, and Angie was surprised to see a petite, woman with long curly hair enter the room. During a previous visit when she'd enquired about Maxine, she had spoken to a male doctor.

"Hi, I'm Dr. Sammoutis," the pretty, tanned woman shook Angie's hand, then Tommy's.

"I'm Detective Inspector Angie North, and this is my partner, Detective Sergeant Tommy O'Brien. I assumed we'd be meeting with Dr. Baldwin."

"Baldwin is on call at the moment, but I'm also Miss Dyer's doctor."

"Okay, what can you tell us?" Angie asked.

"Miss Dyer is suffering from an extreme head trauma. Luckily, early tests show that no brain damage has occurred, although I fear her body will take some time to heal."

"Can we talk to her, Dr. Sammoutis?"

Wearing a lop-sided smile, the woman tilted her head. "She's very weak, Inspector, and her family have asked me to delay a meeting with you. However, Maxine is adamant and keen to speak to the police. I have no choice but to let you see her."

Angie let out a relieved sigh. Tommy was already on his feet, ready to follow her. They walked the length of the corridor and paused when three family members left a private room on the right.

Dr. Sammoutis faced them. "Please, give the patient's family some space. They're very traumatised, you see. Miss Dyer's injuries are a little hard to take right now." The doctor patted Angie on the arm and walked away.

Angie and Tommy waited until the family had left the ward. Then Angie flashed her ID at the officer on guard, tapped on the door, and placed her ear to the wood. She thought she heard a timid voice give them permission to enter. She turned the knob, pushed open the door, and walked in gingerly, with Tommy close behind.

She bit down on her tongue to prevent herself from gasping. The doctor hadn't exaggerated when she'd warned them of Maxine's injuries. As much as Angie wanted to turn away, she knew how unprofessional that would be in front of not only Tommy but the victim too. She walked toward the bed and sat down next to Maxine.

"Hello, Maxine, thanks for agreeing to see us so soon. I'm Detective Inspector Angie North, and this is my partner, Detective Sergeant Tommy O'Brien. We're from the Organised Crime Team," she said softly, her voice full of sympathy.

Maxine's left eye was a ball of purple flesh with a line of dried blood fusing her eyelashes together. Blue bruises covered her jawline and crept up to her lips. Her top lip was red and puffy. Inflamed and discoloured welts were visible on her slim neck above her hospital gown. Angie shuddered to think of the injuries hidden beneath her gown and the sheets.

"Looks bad, eh?" Maxine slurred, her swollen lip hindering her speech.

Angie hesitated, afraid to say the wrong thing to the poor, beaten woman. Tommy, obviously sensing her need for support, quickly joined her at the woman's bedside.

"Physical injuries heal in time, Maxine. You're in the best place. The staff here will have you feeling better in no time at all," Tommy assured the patient with a smile.

Angie was glad of his presence and his warm, caring tone. She thought back to his personal story and wondered how many times his mother had ended up in hospital after a good seeing-to handed out by his brute of a father. Angie cleared the lump in her throat, and Tommy looked down at her. She could only imagine the thoughts that were running through his mind. He prompted her to get back to the task in hand by taking his notebook and pen from his jacket pocket.

"Maxine, I can't tell you how sorry we are that this has happened to you. Are you up to telling us about the attack?"

The woman closed her right eye and sighed. "I've been trawling my mind since I woke up, desperate to remember everything, to give you every piece of information I can."

Angie smiled at the injured woman. "Take your time, Maxine."

When Maxine opened her eye again, a single tear trickled onto her cheek, and she started to recount her ordeal from the moment she'd received the call about her unexpected delivery.

"You've done really well to remember all the details," Angie said, grasping the woman's hand.

"I really didn't have that much in the house. I can't understand why they chose my home to rob, or me, for that matter."

"We already have a lead, Maxine. We're confident we can catch this animal. Is there anything else you remember? Can I ask how many people attacked you?"

"There were two men, but I think only one of them attacked me. Who's to say what went on after I lost consciousness, though?"

"Do you think you could identify either of the two men again?"

"I'm not sure. Once the first man punched me a few times, I felt dizzy, and my vision was blurred. I can't shake the image of his evil eyes glaring at me. I'm sure they were black, the colour of death, staring right at me while he was lying on top of me, grunting and laughing. And that tattoo on his neck—a black beast with yellow eyes. I can see it so clearly now."

Angie looked over her shoulder. Tommy raised his eyes from his notebook and his jaw tightened. They were building a clear picture of the man Chris had identified as Tyler. Angie's interest rose as she listened to the battered woman recount her ordeal in more detail than she thought she'd ever have the courage to do in the same circumstances.

"What can I tell you about the other man? He was tall, white, blond hair. I'd have no hesitation in recognising him, given the chance."

"Did he attack you too?" Even though the woman had been pretty sure he hadn't, Angie knew from experience that the mind played tricks on a person who'd been affected by so much damage.

"Like I said before, I'm pretty sure that he didn't. But I think that's why I could identify him more so. He looked me directly in the eyes, while I pleaded with them to take what they wanted and leave. It was as if he knew what was about to happen to me. He warned me to do as I was told and I wouldn't get hurt, then he walked out of the house. To me, he's as much to blame for my beating as the guy who actually hit me—he did nothing to help. He could have attempted to drag his mate off me. But he did nothing!" Maxine's voice rose. She began to sob and flinched several times as the sharp movements made her wince.

"I know it's difficult. You're safe now. Please, try to keep calm." Angie gripped the woman's hand tighter.

Dr. Sammoutis suddenly barged into the room. "Inspector, I think you've had enough time to question my patient. This is obviously causing Miss Dyer severe discomfort. I must ask you to leave. Now!"

Tommy moved to the door immediately as the doctor rushed over to check Maxine's vital signs on the monitor.

Angie leaned down and whispered in Maxine's ear, "We'll get them, I promise you." She thanked the doctor and left the ward.

Too restless to wait for the lift, Angie briskly descended the stairs.

Tommy struggled to keep up with her. "Boss. Boss. Angie!"

"What!" she screamed and halted mid-step to face him.

"Slow down a minute. You're leaving a trail on fire in your wake."

She balled her hands into fists and inhaled deeply. "I need to knock someone out."

"Go on. I'll let you take one hit, only the one, mind you." He opened his arms wide, leaving his chest exposed for her to strike.

Angie couldn't help but laugh. "Stop it, you prat! I don't mean you."

He chuckled and followed her down the remaining concrete stairs. "I know it's hard to see someone beaten that bad, boss. But that's why we're in this job."

"I know, and I'll make sure we catch every last one of those animals." Tommy stopped walking.

She spun around to face him. "What's wrong?" she asked.

"Well, this is how I see it. We have enough evidence to arrest the two men we believe committed the murders and attacked Maxine, but it's not enough."

"No, because we want to haul in the entire gang."

"Exactly, and I'd wager a hefty bet that those two thugs won't sing like your other man did earlier today."

Angie listened carefully. They'd been lucky with Chris, and she doubted their luck would hold out if they questioned another member of the gang. There was too much at stake, and those thugs usually went down the 'no comment' route once they were tucked up in an interview room. She nodded thoughtfully. "Okay, Tommy. It's time we put your idea in motion. It's time to go undercover, to infiltrate Streetlife."

CHAPTER THIRTEEN

Although the office was occupied by only four people, Angie could sense the surge of energy emanating from her team. A sense of pride wrapped around her shoulders; she felt fortunate to be part of a determined team. At the end of the day, they'd been thrown together by the DCI with one main aim: to create a super-skilled team capable of reducing the organised crime threat within London. And just a few days into the job, they were already working as a unit and uncovering leads that had set them well on the way to a probable arrest. Still, Angie was fully aware of the difficulties that lay ahead of them. Nothing was cut and dried until they had those men sitting in a police cell.

On the way back, Tommy had suggested they pick up supplies from the local bakery. She was beginning to warm to the thoughtful young man. She had an inkling that he was multi-faceted too. Thinking they were in for a spot of overtime that evening, she offered to foot the bill for a tray of tasty delights to accompany the strong coffee on hand in the office.

"Tools down, team," Angie bellowed. "Let's sit together and have a catch-up."

The team were obviously famished. As she placed a tray of pastries on the large table, a swarm of eager hands attacked it.

"Jesus, the apes at Monkey World eat slower than you lot," Tommy joked.

"Some of us have been working our butts off all day around here while you've been out gallivanting with the boss," Jill replied light-heartedly, digging Tommy in the ribs.

They savoured the food for a few minutes in silence. Angie sat back and observed her colleagues one by one, wondering what they were thinking. She knew they had only one way of moving forward and securing a successful arrest. Angie pondered how her team would react under the pressure she was about to place on them. *One way to find out.*

"So, who wants to go first?" Angie asked, once she'd demolished most of her cake.

Jill cleared her throat and wiped the flakes of pastry from her cheek. "I'll go. I looked into the names Chris gave you in his interview. Initially, it was difficult to track them down, what with only having their Christian names to go on. It's a bit of a punt, but these two always seem to be hanging around together, so I'm willing to stake my reputation on it. I think we're after a Tyler Granger and Malcolm 'Malc' Barry. The one thing I'm having difficulty with is finding their connection with the Streetlife gang. They've been in and out of prison for the last ten years, and the rap sheet is long. We're talking robbery, ABH, GBH, possession of hard drugs and stolen goods—"

Tommy let out a low, long whistle. "Sure, they sound like top-notch members of the community."

Jill nodded slowly. "I could go on, but I think you get my drift. Anyway, from what I can gather, they've also been dragged through the foster care system since they were young teenagers. Looks like that's how they met. They seem to have been inseparable ever since, but not related at all. What did strike me as being odd is that they're both in their thirties and not from the Brixton area, from what I can tell, so why would they start at the bottom with this gang? I would've thought they'd be a bit long in the tooth for that."

"These two sound a menace to society," Colin interjected. "My hunch is they probably do it for the kicks. They don't really want to be associated with a gang, as in becoming lifelong members, but they do want to be part of the scams. A case of get what you can and move on."

"I think you might be right. Uncovering their pasts was dead easy as their comings and goings are all well documented," Jill continued. "However, since Tyler's release from Wormwood Scrubs six months ago, the trail dries up. No arrests or cautions for either of them, no known address. They must be getting money from somewhere though, as there is no record of them signing on for benefits."

"Okay, that's good progress," Angie said. "Maxine also confirmed the tattoo on Tyler's neck, so we know it was him and his buddy who attacked her. What have we found out about this gang and the new leader?"

Colin raised his cup in the air while he swallowed what was in his mouth. "That was my job, boss. Duke Mason was the closest member to the ganglord Leroy Charles. However, digging into his past, this Duke has never been arrested. Can you believe that?"

Angie frowned. "I don't understand."

"Duke's had a few warnings over the years, but nothing more. According to social services, his mother was a prostitute. He was brought up in dire conditions until his paternal grandmother offered to care for him. She raised him from the age of six, and not long after she took him in, his mother was found dead from a drug overdose."

"That doesn't explain why he's never been arrested," Angie stated.

"In a way, it does. I guess Duke had somewhere to go, a home and a grandmother who cared for him. He avoided getting caught up in the illegal games the gangs play. Either that, or someone else was watching out for him. If that was the case, my prediction would be that Leroy took him under his wing. I spoke to a friend who works the beat in that area, and he said he'd cautioned Duke a few times in the past, nothing more. When any evidence pointed in his direction another gang member stepped in and confessed to the crime."

"Jesus! So he gets away with *everything*, even murder?" Tommy asked, his eyes widened in disbelief. "He uses the other gang members to do his dirty work and then, if it comes back to bite him on the arse, he gets his lackeys to take the fall instead of him. He's a nasty piece of work."

"That's why he's noted as a person of interest in the system. Uniform have been after him for years, but they can't keep their grasp on him," Colin said. "He might as well drive by the station giving them the finger."

"Then it's down to us to change that, right?" Angie clenched her fist and slammed it down hard on the table, furious that such a lowlife was making a mockery of the justice system, as well as torturing innocent people in the safety of their own homes.

A sensation stirred in the pit of her stomach. Now, more than ever, Angie wanted to show DCI Channing, Scotland Yard and the thugs on the street that she was the right person to front the Organised Crime Team. She was determined that her team would bring the gangs to task. They'd ruled the capital for more years than she could remember. Their violence escalated every year, but now she was in a prime position to put an end to the terror the thugs instilled into innocent people, especially in the Brixton area.

"So what's the plan, boss?" Scott had been quiet, but Angie was pleased to see the light of determination in his eyes.

"Duke Mason is orchestrating these crimes. If we arrest Tyler and Malc now, he'll just replace them with another pair of animals. He'll personally avoid arrest again because we have nothing to connect him to these offences. We need to be clever with our thinking. It would be pointless to swarm in there with all guns blazing. Our aim should be to take down as many Streetlife members as possible. Jill and Frank, I want you both back out on surveillance at Duke's address. We need details, photographs and names of who's coming and going."

"For how long, Angie?" Jill asked.

"A minimum of twenty-four hours. We need to act fast if we're going to arrest Tyler and Malc. It's also imperative for us to find out everything we can about this gang. For all we know, they could have a top brief working for them, so we need to be prepared for that side of things too. If either of those scumbags, Tyler or Malc, turns up at Duke's, we'll put a tail on them straight away. We don't want them out of our sight. Call home, warn your families you won't be home tonight, and then get out there. Once I've updated Channing, Tommy and I will relieve you and take over the nightshift." She glanced at her colleague, and Tommy nodded. "Are you okay with that, Jill and Frank?"

"No problem. Let me call my husband, and I'll be ready to go," Jill said.

Angie hoped Frank's earlier hesitations wouldn't re-emerge. She needed all the team behind the new plan and giving her one hundred percent.

"Boss, I was a bit wary before—it was my first surveillance op—but now we know what these gang members are capable of, I'm fired up and ready to go," Frank assured her.

Angie smiled. "Brilliant. Colin, as you used to work vice in the area, we can't be sure you wouldn't be recognised on the street. So, for now at least, I want you to remain in the office as our base contact."

"Okay, boss. I'll be the go-between and keep you all updated."

She paused. That left Scott to be the one to infiltrate Streetlife. Angie wondered if that would be a problem given that his brother was a drug addict.

"Angie, I can tell you're having reservations," Scott said, dragging her from her thoughts. "While my brother was caught up in the gang culture and it led to his current issues, I'm not him. I'm far stronger than that. Let me use my personal knowledge of gangs and the crimes they commit to become the realistic gang member Streetlife are looking for."

A pang of guilt pierced Angie's heart. "It's not that, Scott. What if you're recognised on the street? You know, through your brother's connection, perhaps? Look, if you're comfortable with going undercover, then who am I to say no? If anyone has any issues with their roles, now is the time to speak up."

The men shook their heads as Jill returned to the group.

"All clear with hubby. Let's nail these bastards," Jill said.

Angie clapped her hands. "Right, I'm off to get the all-clear with Channing. Scott, do your homework on the gang and make sure you're prepped for when the time comes to meet them. Jill and Frank, get out there and keep us updated every time one of those gits so much as sneezes."

Angie was intrigued that no one had asked exactly how Scott would be integrated into Streetlife. She smiled to herself, happy in the knowledge she was always a woman with a plan.

CHAPTER FOURTEEN

Tyler's black four-by-four slowly cruised past the smart terrace houses on Brixton Water Lane. The tinted windows obscured his identity, but it was time for a new ride. Malc had lifted their current car from a supermarket in Clapham two weeks ago, and it had already served its purpose.

Tyler peered around, taking in the scene of easy living and serenity on the street. He enjoyed driving through the calmer neighbourhoods. Less than a mile away from the gritty underground station, markets and graffiti, they were all a stark comparison to real life.

He stomped on the brakes when he stumbled upon what he was looking for. He parked on the corner, a few doors down from number twenty-six, and waited, watching through narrowed eyes.

It was easy to make the call that morning while Malc left the squat for smokes. Tyler had decided he wanted to do the job alone. He hadn't had the freedom to enjoy himself in months. Malc annoyed him by always questioning his motives and imploring him to stop, and now he had Duke on his back, playing God, dishing out orders and jobs. He'd found it easy to discreetly jot down the extra mobile number from Dev's list the last time he'd visited the flat. When he'd rung the woman, she'd given out her personal details freely. *Stupid bitch!* She'd told him that she was expecting a parcel, but wouldn't be home until three that afternoon. As an added bonus, her address was just around the corner from where he was staying. That kind of deal, he found hard to resist.

Tyler took a pack of tissues from his pocket and thoroughly wiped every surface he had touched. He shoved the used tissues back into his coat and slipped on his black leather gloves. With the keys still in the ignition, he climbed out of the car and made his way up the street.

The stone, three-storey townhouses with white-painted bay window panes increased Tyler's anger. The trimmed hedges and tidy front lawns, decorated with colourful flowerbeds or a disregarded child's toy, reminded him of what he'd never had. Since he was thirteen, Tyler had been shunted from home to home, forced to live with a different family each month. Envy was a powerful emotion for someone who'd suffered the way he had.

He quickly scanned the area then rushed up the path to the front door. It was deserted, more like walking up a country lane rather than approaching a house in an over-populated postcode. He poised his gloved finger over the bell, sneaking one last glance over his shoulder. With the coast all clear, he rang the bell.

"Just a second!" a voice called out from the other side of the glossy red door.

"Johnston's Courier Service," he bellowed in reply, realising he'd left the fake parcel in the car.

Fuck it! Oh well, it's not like I really need it anyway.

A beautiful woman, wearing a wrap-over flowery dress that accentuated every curve, opened the door. Long, blonde curls bounced over her shoulders, and her smile was sugary sweet. "Hi."

After being momentarily distracted by her beauty, Tyler snapped into action. "Fiona Morrell?"

"That's right. Did we speak on the phone earlier?" She looked down at his empty hands. "Where's my parcel?"

Not bothering to come up with a suitable excuse, he launched at her, shoving her roughly back into the house. He kicked the door, and it slammed shut. The noise echoed through the empty hallway.

"What are you doing?" she stuttered, shuffling back towards the wall, trying to shake off his firm grasp.

He ignored her. His eyes roamed her body, from her generously sized breasts down to the hem of her dress. When his eyes finally met hers, he licked his lips and waited for her to scream, for the shrill of fear to turn him on.

Instead, she slapped him around the face and took off down the narrow hallway, towards the back of the house. Tyler's nostrils flared in annoyance as he drew in a lungful of hot air. He hated it when they played the cat-and-mouse game. Realising she was heading for the mobile phone lying on the kitchen table, he jumped on her back. He grabbed a handful of tousled locks and yanked her head back. She screamed, grappling for the phone. He knocked it out of her hand, dropped it on the stone floor, and smashed it with the heel of his boot.

"Please, just tell me what you want! Take anything! I won't stop you."

Tyler sneered. "I don't need permission, bitch. I *will* take what I want."

He pushed her towards the centre island of the large kitchen. Her body trembled as parts of her connected with his chest and groin. His power over her turned him on; his erection grew at her vulnerability. He bent her over with such force, her head cracked against the oak worktop. Tyler's hand shot under her dress, eager to feel her bare, milky flesh, but he couldn't risk removing his gloves. Not yet. As he ripped down her underwear, she remained motionless. He undid the button on his worn, bleached-washed jeans, but stopped when he heard a murmur. Unable to figure out the location of the noise, he scanned every corner of the room, apprehension making him suck in a breath. *Shit, is someone else home? Am I about to get caught?* The quiet descended once more, and the necessity to finish what he'd started took over.

"Mama! Mama! Mama!" The voice sounded as though it had come from inside a tin can. It was then he saw the white plastic baby monitor sitting close to the sink. The dial flashed intermittently between green and red every time the child made a noise.

"Plea-please—" The woman's voice was barely audible. "Please don't hurt my daughter."

A child wasn't about to prevent him from having his fun. He thrust down his boxer shorts, gripped her waist tightly with both hands, and shrugged as his penis entered her.

CHAPTER FIFTEEN

The meeting with DCI Channing went according to plan, which was gratifying for Angie. He had agreed with the intricacies of the operation and offered all the support and resources the team needed to complete the task.

Aware of the time constraints, Angie rushed back to the team to bring them up to speed. But first, she found a quiet spot in the corridor and quickly contacted her husband to update him.

"Hello, sweetie," Warren said.

"It's so good to hear your voice." Angie sighed and leaned against the wall.

"I take it this phone conversation, and not seeing you walk through the front door, means you're working late?"

Angie smiled. *There's no fooling him after all these years.* "I'm sorry, darling. I know we said we'd make an effort to make date night work, but the case has become more urgent. We've set up a surveillance op—two colleagues are out there now—and I've volunteered to do the nightshift—"

"Say no more!"

"Really? You're not mad?"

"Yes, really." He laughed. "I know you wouldn't do it if it wasn't totally necessary. You were a workaholic from day one, remember? I love you anyway."

She could hear the smile radiating in his words and was tempted to rearrange her team's roles so she could rush home—first to dig him in the ribs then to hug him for having such an understanding nature.

"Angie, stay safe out there."

"I always do."

"Right, well, it's boys' night for us then. I might even treat Luke to a takeaway."

"If you can get him out of his room, you mean?"

"Stop worrying. He's a young lad; he'll come round. I used to be locked away in my room at his age."

"That's enough, Mr. North. We both know exactly what you would've been up to!"

The pair said goodbye and hung up. After chatting with Warren, Angie was filled with renewed vigour. The thought of Luke becoming a troubled teenager and being tempted into a lawless existence by the likes of Streetlife spurred her on. A determined woman on a mission, she strode into the office to find everyone hard at work.

Tommy turned his chair to face her. "Jill and Frank are in place. Everything seems quiet at Mason's address."

"Thanks, Tommy. Do they know if Duke is there?"

"He sure is. Arrived a few hours ago with another black male. Jill managed to get a photo of the unidentified associate and sent it via MMS. I ran it through facial recognition—no match. Colin's putting the call out to his contacts to see if any of them can put a name to the face."

Colin waved at Angie, too busy on the phone to update her himself.

"Okay, well, it's still progress," she said. "It's seven p.m. Let's head to the canteen for a bite to eat, and we'll take over surveillance at nine."

"Works for me, Angie. I could eat a scabby horse."

She shuddered at the image he'd conjured up.

"It means I'm so hungry I'd eat anything right now."

"Yeah, I got that, Tommy." She shook her head and walked across the room to Scott, who was surrounded by paperwork. "Everything okay?"

"All good, boss. Just getting up to speed with the Brixton area, the different gangs, and my story for the undercover op. Has the chief approved it?"

"He has. He's behind us one hundred percent. Will you join us for a comfort break?"

"Great idea. I get tetchy if I skip a meal," he said, smiling.

Angie admired the amount of research Scott had completed. She wondered if he'd called his fiancée but decided against asking him. The last thing she wanted was to come across as the team's mother. Colin was still on the phone, speaking in a hushed tone, but she motioned that they were going to get something to eat. He shook his head. *I'll bring him back a sandwich.*

Angie, Tommy and Scott joined the queue in the busy canteen and placed their order. Angie was stunned to hear a familiar voice among the numerous officers having a break. DI David Meadows's unmistakeable cockney tone was impossible to ignore.

She turned around tentatively, hoping her ears had deceived her. They hadn't. The man's loud voice drowned out the rest of the men he was sitting with at a nearby table. During their training days at Hendon, Angie had always regarded the outspoken fool as her nemesis.

Over the years, their paths had crossed on numerous occasions. The last time was at her previous station in Fulham when Meadows had been appointed to cover a DI on sick leave. Angie rarely used the term *hate*, especially where other officers were concerned, but it was difficult for her to come up with another suitable word for how she felt about David Meadows.

Although neither of them had stepped out of line professionally, Meadows had a habit of winding her up at every opportunity. On a number of occasions, she'd been tempted to slap his arrogant face. There was definitely a mutual disdain between them. Angie put his arrogance down to professional envy. Meadows was the type of guy who didn't appreciate a female officer leaping ahead of him. She had heard on the grapevine that he'd applied to be part of the Organised Crime Team, and she had breathed a relieved sigh when he'd got turned down.

A low whistle escaped Meadows's lips. "Well, well, well... if it isn't Angie North."

Angie ignored his antagonising tone. "Inspector Meadows. I thought I heard your bellowing voice."

"Showing off your detective skills, are we?" He nudged the man closest to him.

The man looked awkward and didn't respond.

"Thankfully, I don't have to sink to your level and use sarcasm, Inspector Meadows." Her taut smile never wavered. She could sense her two colleagues watching the interaction with interest. The woman behind the counter placed their meals on their trays, then Angie paid and strode past Meadows. "Enjoy your meal, *gentlemen*."

The three of them sat at the only free table, which happened to be a few feet away from her nemesis. She leaned forward and whispered, "Pretend you didn't witness that."

"I think you'll find I just made an arrest," Meadows hollered, but Angie chose to ignore him. "A domestic murder," he continued, his voice rising another level.

She wondered if he was intent on provoking her or whether he always showed off when he made an arrest, as they were such a rarity.

"Who is that gobshite?" Tommy whispered.

Angie couldn't help but laugh. "Let's put it this way… he's not someone I usually put on my Christmas card list."

While her two colleagues grinned, her interest was drawn enough that she turned her head, hoping to catch Meadows's bragging tale.

"Good on yer, David. Where did all this kick off then?" one of the men in Meadows's group asked.

"Some town house in Brixton. The husband tried to make it look like a robbery, but he was covered in her blood, and there was no forced entry. Their kid was crying in her cot upstairs when I got there—"

"When did this happen?" Angie demanded.

"What?" Meadows frowned, seemingly annoyed at the interruption.

"When was the crime committed? When did you make an arrest?"

"This afternoon."

Angie's heart thumped against her ribs. "Was anything taken from the house?"

Meadows ignored her and continued to revel in the attention bestowed upon him. "The husband kept yelling, 'It wasn't me! It wasn't me'. Tried to tell me that someone else had been there. But come on. His hands were covered in her blood."

"What was taken, Meadows?" Angie's cheeks burned as her temper mounted.

He sighed deeply. "Some cash, allegedly—"

"It wasn't the husband," Angie said vehemently.

"Stop interrupting me, for Christ's sake!"

Angie twisted in her chair and looked directly at Tommy. "We need to look into this. Alarm bells are ringing in my ears. I have a suspicion this is the work of our gang."

Meadows rose to his feet. "You'll do no such thing, lady. This is my case."

"Detective Inspector North will suffice," she shouted, her temper finally exploding.

"It's *my* case, and *I've* apprehended the suspect, DI North."

"It's a complex case. If you just let us have a look—"

"No one will be sticking their oar into my case." Meadows inched closer to Angie.

Tommy and Scott shot out of their chairs to form a barricade.

He eyed the two younger men with hatred. "So back off!" Spittle flew from his mouth, and he rejoined his group.

Angie pushed her tray to the centre of the table, her appetite lost, and she left the table. Tommy and Scott followed her out of the canteen before another war of words erupted.

"Sorry if I came across as unprofessional back there, guys. That clown always brings out the worst in me."

"Understandable. He seems a right dickhead. There's definitely no reason for you to apologise," Tommy said.

She appreciated his reassurance, but her personal disappointment was harder to ignore. "He's wrong. I know we haven't looked into the case yet, but my gut feeling is that the husband didn't do this."

"We still need to be cautious."

"Spit it out, Tommy. What are you getting at?"

"Angie, we're involved in the Organised Crime Team! From what I can tell, we have information that surpasses what's available to others in the force, including this DI Meadows fellow, so if he wants to go down the domestic violence route, let him."

"I can't let an innocent man take the blame for killing his wife, Tommy, not when the cases are so similar. Maybe I should go higher, ask Channing to get the case notes for us to look at."

"Either way, it's too late for us to save the woman now. We should concentrate on the plan we have in place, the surveillance and undercover op. Make sure no one else is harmed. We can look into Meadows's case once we've caught the gang."

Although she was shocked by Tommy's forthright tone, his words held the truth. "Okay, you have a point. I'll let you have that one."

He smiled broadly.

"But! I still want the case notes on that murder so we can pin it on the gang."

Tommy winked. "It's not a battle to fight today, boss. That's all I'm saying. That DI seems set in his ways, and it would take up a lot of our valuable time to combat his obtuse attitude."

"You noticed that about him, eh?" She smiled for the first time since laying eyes on Meadows. "I'll pass it on to Colin. Leave him to square it with the chief, and then he can dig into the case, see if my instincts are right."

"I'm sure there's no doubt about that, Angie," Scott chipped in.

Pushing the confrontation with Meadows to the very back of her mind, she led them back to the office. Her first priority was to oversee the undercover plan. With someone on the inside, she felt confident another victim's life wouldn't be traumatised by the gang.

CHAPTER SIXTEEN

The night air was humid and sticky. The promise of a hot summer lay on the horizon. Angie cracked open the window, hoping for a breath of fresh air. Nothing came. The clock on the dashboard said it was three minutes to eleven, and all was quiet on the Brixton estate they were surveying. Duke Mason's front room window, on the sixth floor, was illuminated. Music thumped through the open window, with little consideration for the neighbours. During the surveillance, no one had either entered or left the flat.

They had relieved Jill and Frank at nine thirty, slightly later than anticipated. Jill and Frank covered their disappointment well. She sent them home to recharge their batteries. By the looks of things, they were in for a quiet night.

Angie had assumed her partner would be the chatty type during surveillance, passing the time with stories and anecdotes, but Tommy seemed rather pensive and barely spoke. He sat upright and alert, his camera poised and ready for action. Angie thought back to the day they met, which somehow seemed like months ago rather than days. She wondered if his determination to catch criminals and serve justice was born from his inability to help his own mother during her abusive marriage to his father.

She cupped her hands over her face and rubbed vigorously. Uncertainty coursed through her veins. *Are we doing the right thing?* Apart from one potential gang member, Jill and Frank hadn't uncovered any new leads or probable allies of Duke Mason. She had an inkling that she and Tommy were facing a night of the same fate:

fruitless hours where nothing of significance came their way. She doubted whether integrating Scott into the violent gang was the right course for them to take. Wouldn't the rational decision be to arrest Tyler and Malc? Or maybe it would be wiser to investigate the gang more thoroughly. Tommy soon interrupted her thoughts.

"Heads up, Angie! Get a load of this," he said, snapping a succession of photos.

Two white men appeared out of a dark alley and headed for the block of flats. Even in the limited light from the few available streetlights, Angie could make out the large tattoo on the taller man's neck.

"Get a picture of that, Tommy."

"I'm on it! Probably won't be the best picture, but it's obvious what we're looking at," he said while peering at the camera screen.

"Brilliant! That's our guys then. Tyler Granger and his buddy Malc Barry. This is what we've been waiting for."

"Cocky shits. Strolling along without a care in the world."

Angie frowned. "You're right. Where's their car? Everyone we've spoken to has described a black four-by-four. But here they are, on foot."

"Maybe they parked around the corner?" Tommy grunted and continued to take photos of the men entering the tower block.

"Here's the plan!" Her urgency forced Tommy to stop snapping. "We get in contact with Colin and Scott at the office—Scott is still there, isn't he?"

"Yep, he's spoken to his fiancée and explained he'll be away from home for a while."

"That's good. It makes sense—he'll be putting in a lot of extra hours until we finish this case. Right, tell Colin to get down here now! I want these two followed once they've left Mason's flat. He needs to be careful in his pursuit in case they have abandoned their car or something."

"Okay, what about Scott?"

"He can get on the wires, see if there are any reports of either stolen or abandoned four-by-four cars. Get him to look into the CCTV footage of the area too."

"Leave it with me." Tommy reached for his mobile phone.

Angie retrieved the camera from his lap and started thumbing through the stills of the thugs. The men's few seconds of movements in front of them played out across a hundred shots.

* * *

Duke was slouched on the sofa, his head tilted back and his eyes closed. The music ran through his body, and he swayed to the lyrics of Jay Z, dreaming of a better life. He couldn't care less about the fame—he craved the money and power, the freedom to do as he wanted without fear of repercussions.

He heard a loud thud on the door, and his eyes flew open; there was only one person it could be. The wisdom of Jay Z's words wasn't lost on him as he crossed the room to open the door: *'I've got ninety-nine problems, but a bitch ain't one.'*

Duke grumbled, "It's this guy causing all my problems right now."

"Yeah, I bet you wishing it was bitches you had to deal with," Dev said.

"Real talk. Though thinking about it, these white dudes are like little bitches."

"Yeah, and we gotta cut them loose." Dev agreed, rolling up his joint.

Duke walked into the dark hallway separating the living room and front door. He clenched his fists a number of times to keep his temper in check. The bang against the glass was more persistent the second time. He narrowed his eyes as his anger bubbled inside. Realising he needed to be smart, he calmed himself by taking a deep breath. Even though he was tempted to knock seven bells out of the men, thoughts of how Leroy would have handled the situation were prominent in his mind. He needed to be patient and ensure his name was not connected to the two idiots standing outside his flat.

He opened the door and snarled.

"What's up, man?" Tyler brushed past Duke and into the flat.

Malc grinned awkwardly and, unlike Tyler, waited for permission to enter.

Duke nodded slightly.

The three of them walked into the living room. *Keep it calm. Don't let this fucker see your anger.*

Duke threw himself onto the sofa. "So, what you boys up to?"

"You know, just chilling," Tyler said, bobbing his head to the music.

Duke cringed at the ease and confidence exuding from the man.

Tyler perched on the armchair and leaned forward with his arms resting on his knees.

"Quiet day?" Duke asked.

"Yeah, done fuck all, and now we're bored."

"Nothing happening here tonight, boys. Why don't ya check out The Corner House? I'm sure there's a game on."

"We ain't interested in cards!" Tyler snapped.

"Easy, it was just a suggestion." Duke enjoyed provoking the man.

"C'mon, Duke, you must have something for us."

"Hmm, I dunno. We need to stall it for a bit. Don't want to hit too many places. People start asking questions, you know?"

"Nah, man, don't worry about that. We're in and out quick. Ain't no one seeing us."

The man laughed hard, and Duke grunted. It was obvious the pair, or Tyler at least, was not up to date with the news. *Or is he, and just doesn't care?* Duke cussed himself, furious he didn't know more about the men. Leroy would have jumped all over him for being so slack.

"Fuck it, why not! Take a couple of new numbers. We've had them a while, just ain't hit them yet."

"What?" Dev shouted.

Duke bore his eyes into Dev's, silencing his friend. The last thing he wanted was to raise Tyler's suspicions that he was on to him. "Give them the numbers. That stuff has gone to your head, man." He nodded at the joint Dev was smoking.

"What's the problem?" Tyler asked, his left leg juddering, out of sync with the music.

There were a few moments of heated silence. Duke gritted his teeth, waiting for Dev to get his act together.

"Nah, nothing. Don't mind me; just a bit stoned." Dev laughed and handed Tyler the joint. The man accepted and pulled hard on the Rizla.

"This is good shit," Tyler said, letting out a puff of dark-grey smoke.

Duke relaxed. For the moment, he was satisfied Dev had understood his message and that Tyler had no idea of the game they were playing.

Dev went over to his desk and returned with a sheet of paper; he exchanged it with Tyler for his spliff. Tyler jumped up eagerly and handed the details to Malc. The man hopped from one foot to the other, while his partner slipped the paper into his black leather jacket.

"Cool, man." Tyler faced Duke. "We're gonna make a move, call some numbers."

"It's late, man. A bit suss to be getting a call from a delivery company at this time of night."

"I didn't mean now. You think we're amateurs or something?" Tyler roared with laughter and jabbed Malc in the ribs.

Duke got the impression Tyler was laughing at him, and his blood boiled again. *The sooner this guy is out of my flat, the better.* "Good to hear."

"Well, we're out! Catch you tomorrow once we've made the hit."

"That's cool, bruv. Take your time. We trust you," Duke said, the words tripping off his tongue.

Tyler grinned and fist-bumped Duke and Dev before leaving the room. The ever-quiet Malc followed his pal like a sheep following a shepherd. When the front door slammed, Duke moved over to the window.

"What the fuck, man?" Dev spat.

Duke ignored him. He was expecting his mate to question him.

"Seriously, I told you I weren't down for this shit. Murdering innocent women in their homes ain't on."

"Cool it, Dev. You gave them old numbers, right?"

"Yeah, they were the first set of numbers. Those houses were raided by Feral and Ace already."

"Good, you understood my message. What you so worried about then?"

"Those two imbeciles don't know that, though, do they? They're gonna rock up to houses that—"

"Will probably be fitted with extra security by now."

"You don't know that, Duke," Dev cried, his exasperation evident.

"No, I fucking don't! But we'll just have to think that for now."

"I still ain't happy with it, man. Them two are fucking nuts."

Duke peered down from his elevated position and watched the two men sneak into the darkness. It was all quiet on his patch; not many people dared to step foot outside their door after dark. Duke would have preferred to parade the streets at night, exuding his power, but that wasn't going to happen this evening. Tyler and Malc had destroyed his buzz and left him with the stale taste of irritation.

The two men dipped into the alley and out of Duke's view. He needed to devise a plan quickly to remove them from his gang permanently, but the drugs were addling his brain.

"At the end of the day, dear friend of mine," Duke said, his eyes fixed on the murky backstreet, "I have to think of myself first. Let them two fuck things up. The police are looking for them, not me. And that's the way I plan on keeping it."

CHAPTER SEVENTEEN

Most of the team gathered around the large conference table. Angie grinned at DCI Channing, pleased that he'd taken the time to join them. So far, he'd let her do all the talking. It was important that everyone understood the brief and what was expected of them before the undercover operation began.

"Officer Jones is escorting Chris Strange up here now. I wanted to make sure everyone is comfortable with the op. Any problems, speak up now." Angie's gaze skipped around the team. They all seemed contemplative, and she wondered if they were worried about Scott going undercover.

As if reading her mind, Scott cleared his throat. "I'll be fine. Don't look so worried, people. All the background checks have been made, and I've worked out my story. I'll be going in as Chris Strange's cousin, new to the area and desperate to see some action. Let's see if that's enough to get me involved first, and then we can develop the sting operation."

"Scott's right," Angie said, standing at the head of the table. "We can't let this opportunity pass us by. Duke Mason has slipped through the Met's fingers too often in the past. From this point, Scott will be working under the assumed name of Todd Strange."

Angie handed Scott a cheap prepaid phone and a wallet containing a fake driving licence. She couldn't tell if his expression showed concern or if he was piecing things together in his mind. She hoped it was the latter.

"If you send us any messages, make sure you delete them straight away," Tommy reminded Scott. "Always erase your call log. For emergencies, I've programmed my personal mobile number in your contacts as Tom Buyer."

"Cheers, mate." Scott's light-hearted tone belied seriousness.

Angie brushed aside her concerns and continued with the briefing. "Thanks to DCI Channing, we've been granted extra resources for the operation, Scott. You will be followed at all times, never far from our sight."

"What about the tail on Tyler and Malc?" Scott queried.

"Jill and Frank are out there now. Colin, before Chris joins us, do you want to give us a quick update on what occurred when you put the pair under surveillance last night?"

"Sure thing, boss. After leaving Mason's flat, the pair remained on foot. I ditched my car too. They led me to a council estate on Villa Road approximately twenty minutes from Mason's place. It seems like a squat to me. I stayed there for an hour or so. They didn't leave the property again, so I returned to base."

Angie needed to keep all the balls up in the air, maintaining surveillance on the suspects as well as organising the sting operation. Now she had the added headache of dealing with Meadows too. She turned to face Channing, who winked at her and urged her on. "We have to remember we can arrest these two lowlifes at any moment, but we also need them as bait to catch Duke. I've told Jill and Frank to stick to the fuckers like glue. Scott, did you find out any more about the black four-by-four?"

"Yes. A vehicle matching that description was stolen from Clapham a few weeks ago. Not sure if it'll prove anything if we believe they're switching the plates after each job."

"Get in touch with Jill and Frank. Maybe they can tell us what vehicle the men are using now, if they're using one. These guys might have realised we're on to them and ditched it. Perhaps they'll be on the lookout for something new to use instead. And, Colin, as you're staying here—"

"I'm on it, boss. I'll search the relevant CCTV footage and the ANPR system, see if anything crops up."

A knock on the door halted their conversation. Officer Jones entered the room with a sheepish-looking Chris Strange in tow. Although Strange wasn't in handcuffs, the way his leather jacket was hanging off his right shoulder, indicated that probably Jones had dragged him up the stairs roughly. Angie offered the young man the seat nearest to Scott. Chris appeared vulnerable and less cocky than he had in the interview room.

"Chris, meet Todd Strange," she said, gesturing to Scott. "He's your long-lost cousin from your father's side. He's just moved in with you. Todd will be tied to your waist, figuratively speaking, at all times until this is over. That includes staying at your flat."

The young man shifted uncomfortably in his chair. He gazed at Scott through untrusting eyes. His expression didn't exactly fill Angie with confidence.

"Okay," he mumbled.

"Chris, this is a serious operation we are implementing," DCI Channing said, speaking for the first time. "If you expect us to keep our side of the deal, to protect you and fulfil our offer of a reduced sentence, possibly immunity, then we need to ensure we can trust you. Are you up to this?"

"Well... yes. I am... I mean—"

"Speak up, son," Channing bellowed.

Heavy tension blanketed the room. Expectant faces glared at Chris. A sudden need to reassure him overwhelmed Angie. She walked around the table and pulled out the vacant chair next to Chris. "Listen, I appreciate that you're nervous, apprehensive even."

"Damn right, I am. I'm the one in the shit if Duke finds out."

"If you play this right, Duke won't find out until he's banged up for years." Her motherly instinct taking over, she reached out to touch his hand gently. "We'll have officers tailing you and Todd at all times, ready to pounce at the first sign of trouble."

"Okay..." Chris paused, then spoke assertively. "I need the loot your lot took off me when I was arrested. If I turn up at Duke's house empty-handed, it won't matter who's with me; none of us will be getting out of his gaff without a beating."

"That's all in hand, Chris. You'll have the money, plus some extra cash that you would've made from the jewellery sale." Angie rose from the table.

"And you'll tell Duke I helped you sell the gear, all right?" Scott said sternly.

Angie wondered if he used the same tone of voice when he spoke to his younger brother.

With everyone clear about their duties, the team dispersed. It was all down to Chris and Todd Strange to gather the evidence they needed to bring Duke Mason in.

CHAPTER EIGHTEEN

Scott pulled up and cut the engine on the car he'd been assigned for the operation. Peering through the window, he felt small, fenced in by the neglected high-rise flats. He doubted the sun had shown the place any love over the years. The prominent obscene graffiti and piss-stained pavements were signs of the gang members marking their territory.

Being the only officer who hadn't entered the estate yet, Scott realised the photographs hadn't done the place any form of justice. The still images had failed to capture the cold atmosphere and sinister mood. He watched a group of lads, all wearing dark hoodies, walking past and kicking a beer can between them. Just sitting in the car, he felt intimidated. He dreaded to think of how the neighbours felt living here.

An image of his younger brother, Ross, flashed through his mind. They had grown up on an estate in northwest London, granted not half as bad as this one, but they had both chosen very different paths in life. He'd started working in a bank, where he'd met his fiancée, before he managed to secure a role in the police force. His choices had led to a career, wedding plans and a semi-detached house in Richmond. That was the total opposite of how estate life and gang culture had enticed his naïve brother, who was reliant on drugs. He shook his head to discard the memories.

Chris sat beside him, scrolling through Facebook on his phone. The nerves fluttered in Scott's stomach, but thinking of Ross spurred him on. This was his chance to prove to the team he was up to the job.

"What are you doing wasting time on your fucking phone?" Scott yelled, taking to his role as if he'd always been a gang member.

"Chill, man! I'm ready when you are."

"Are you *sure* you're ready for this?"

"Yep, I don't intend doing time for no one."

Scott had to believe the lad was genuine, though he still had a niggling doubt Chris wasn't being truthful with the team. On the other hand, maybe this opportunity was all Chris needed to get back on the right path. Scott's own brother had been branded a grass in the past, so he knew exactly what was at stake for Chris.

"Okay, let's play this cool tonight and see how we get on. Any sign of trouble, we leg it, all right?"

Chris shrugged and exited the car. Scott followed, hanging back a little to make sure anyone who was observing them knew Scott understood his place as the new kid on the estate. Chris pulled open the heavy rusting door, its green paint peeling away from the frame. Inside the building, the smell of cannabis instantly assaulted Scott's nose. The group of hooded youths who had passed the car moments before were casually strewn across the bottom of the stairwell, smoking and laughing.

"Hey, bruv, where you been? Ain't seen you around lately." A black teenager stood up and fist-bumped Chris.

"Sorting stuff for Duke. You know how it is, man."

The mere mention of Duke's name forced the group to their feet and out of Chris's way. Scott couldn't help but wonder if Chris held more influence than he had led the task force to believe. The pair climbed the stairs in silence until they reached the sixth floor.

"Don't speak too much. It pisses Duke right off," Chris said over his shoulder. "And don't get cocky—he hates that too."

Scott welcomed the warning. Although he'd conducted as much research as he could on Streetlife, those nuggets of information could only come from insiders.

Chris pounded on the door. Seconds later, a small mixed-race kid, no more than sixteen, flung open the door. He held a joint in one hand and a can of beer in the other.

"Yo, Chris! Where you been, man? Dev's been asking around for you."

"All right, Billy? This is Todd, my cousin," Chris replied, as though the explanation would be sufficient. He pushed past the boy and walked into the flat.

Billy looked Scott up and down then laughed. His eyes were red and glazed. Scott wanted to slap the kid around the head and send him home to his mother.

"Come in, man!" Billy said once he'd stopped laughing.

Scott eased himself into the flat. The smell of cannabis was becoming more familiar and less of a shock to his senses. Voices bellowed from the nearest room, and Scott quickened his pace before stopping short of the door.

"Who the fuck is that?" a tall black man asked as he marched towards Scott.

"Chill, Duke! That's my cousin, Todd."

"Well, I didn't invite him here. What's he doing in my fuckin' house?"

"I've told you, he's my cuz. What's the problem?" Chris mumbled.

Duke stopped in front of Chris and glared at him. His six-foot frame towered over Chris's small, skinny figure. Scott was tempted to step in, to diffuse the situation, but Chris's earlier caution prevented him.

"I asked you a fucking question!" Duke stepped closer to Chris, bending down within inches of the lad's face.

"Come on, man. He's cool. He's family. He even helped me shift the loot."

"He's not *my* fucking family. Why's he touching *my* gear?"

Duke's nostrils flared. His biceps protruded through the Nike T-shirt, and Scott knew it would take only one punch from the man to put Chris on his arse. Aware that he would blow his cover if he intervened, Scott mentally urged Chris to man up.

Chris finally found his voice again. "Leroy said it would be cool."

Duke drew in a deep breath, his large chest growing in size and power. "What did you just say? Who said you could bring his name into this?"

"Hey, Duke, I didn't mean any harm."

Duke grabbed Chris by the neck of his T-shirt and threw him against the wall. Before Scott had a chance to react, the other occupant in the room, another black man, ran at the pair and stood between them.

"Dev, back off! This piece of scum can't come in my yard, talking about Leroy."

"Easy, Duke! You asked the boy a question. Let him answer."

Scott observed the interaction, feeling helpless but curious about the relationship between Duke and his right-hand man, Dev, whom he now recognised from the photo Frank had taken during surveillance.

Duke relented and released Chris. He straightened out the boy's clothes. "You're lucky Dev likes you. I'll give you a minute to explain yourself."

The fear in Chris's eyes was obvious. Scott slipped his hand inside his jacket pocket and wrapped his fingers around the mobile phone, ready to hit Tommy's number sooner than he'd thought he would need to.

"I was just saying that Leroy was happy for me to bring friends round once in a while. He trusted me. I'd made arrangements for him to meet Todd before he... well you know, left us. I just assumed if Leroy was cool with my cuz swinging by, it would be sweet with you. I wouldn't disrespect you, man."

Chris looked Duke in the eye for a second or two before glancing down at his feet. The boy had stepped up to the plate and played the wounded puppy-dog routine well. Scott dropped his hand at his side and suppressed a snigger when Duke's defences melted.

Duke howled suddenly, and everyone in the room, except for Dev, jumped in surprise. He slapped an arm round Chris's shoulder, pulled him close, and rubbed the boy's head with his knuckles. Dev laughed and returned to the sofa.

"So, what's your name?" Duke studied Scott, a smile spreading across his face, his arm still locked tightly around Chris.

"Todd," Scott said, gulping, feigning nervousness.

"Oh, er, Todd! How very posh." Duke released Chris from his grasp.

Dev, Chris and Billy laughed loudly in unison. Scott joined in, not wanting to offend the giant of a man on their first meeting. Duke walked towards him, studying every inch of his face.

"Well, if Leroy was cool with you coming here, then you're welcome, man." Duke extended his fist.

Scott's fist connected with Duke's as relief flooded through him.

"Come on, sit down and get comfortable. We were just testing out some new gear."

"Before Chris gets his hands on this new shit, he better have something for us," Dev said, concentrating on the joint he was rolling.

"Don't be stupid, man. I told you, Todd helped me shift the last bits." Chris unloaded a wedge of notes from his pocket and threw them on the coffee table.

Dev spread the money across the table. "Yeah, that looks fine. Here, try this." He handed Chris the smoke.

Scott sat down cautiously, hoping to keep the attention off himself, but he knew Duke was still watching him from the corner of his eye while he stood at the window.

"So, *Todd*, how come you were so useful to Chris?"

"Oh, you know how it is; I know people."

"People we don't?" Duke challenged him.

"Call me the middle man. I have contacts all over London, but I never get caught. That's why I'm useful." Scott could tell he'd stimulated Duke's interest. "I don't get caught up in the dirty side of things. How you get the loot is your business. But I know how to sell, and there's always someone willing to buy. I use different people to shift things. That's why the pigs never get their hands on me."

Duke laughed. The beeping of a phone interrupted their conversation. Scott felt he'd said enough to impress the leader, for the moment at least.

"Oh, fuck!" Dev shouted.

"What is it, man?" Duke demanded.

"It's that fuckin' nurse from the hospital."

"What about her? What's she saying?"

The tension returned to Duke's face, and Scott pretended to be disinterested as he took the joint from Chris.

"She said that Maxine woman was released from the ward today," Dev said, looking at the screen. "She's already spoken to the police and left the hospital."

"We need to sort this! It was Tyler and Malc's hit, so they've got the woman's address, and we can't exactly ask them for it." Duke paused, placing a hand on his chin. "Get your nurse friend to grab it from the hospital records," he finally demanded.

"What? Nah, I'm not happy with that."

"Just fuckin' do it!" Duke's eyes bore into Dev, and Scott got the impression the man didn't want to discuss it with a room full of people. "We'll pay her a visit tomorrow."

Dev groaned and typed a text message in reply. Scott was still holding the rolled-up cigarette and could feel Duke's eyes burning into him. He had little option but to take a drag. The heat of the tobacco burnt his throat, and the cannabis affected his head instantly. He coughed and urged Chris to relieve him of the joint.

"Good shit, right," Duke said. He laughed as the heat enflamed Scott's face.

"Yeah, it's good," Scott choked.

"Right, boys! Let's roll another one and turn up the beats. Billy, get everyone a beer."

The mood in the room was a stark contrast to the one that had greeted them moments before. Scott broke out in a sweat, unsure if it was the effects of the illegal substance or his desperation to get in touch with his team. Chris eased back into his role of cocky gang member, necking back the beers with the others. Scott was on tenterhooks in case Chris snitched on him. He moved to the edge of the sofa and whispered in the lad's ear.

"Your old mum never teach you whispering is rude, man?" Duke called out over the music.

Scott laughed. "Sorry, man, just letting Chris know that I'm stepping outside to make a call."

"For what? You can talk freely in front of us."

Duke's tone was light. However, Scott's nerves were taut when he spotted the way the leader was frowning.

"Nah, it's to my girl, innit. If she hears the music, you lot... well, it ain't worth the aggro."

"Ha! Are you serious, Toddy boy? You answer to your *woman*?"

He remained silent.

Everyone in the room stared at him, keen to hear his response.

He shrugged helplessly. "Nah, of course not."

"Good! Turn your damn phone off. There's no hoes over bros in this house. You get me?" Duke roared with laughter and passed his joint to Scott.

Billy handed Scott another can of beer. If he objected, it would only cause suspicion. He switched off his phone and placed it on the table. Both hands free, Scott accepted the joint and raised his can in the air. Duke looked appeased by his actions and relaxed back in his chair.

Scott pulled hard on the joint, managing to control the suffocating sensation of the smoke, and washed it down with a gulp of beer.

Damn! I need to warn the team about Maxine.

CHAPTER NINETEEN

Maxine was in her living room, cowering on the sofa, with her knees pulled tightly under her chin. She was petrified of being alone so soon after being discharged from the hospital. Unfortunately, her parents had booked a Caribbean cruise that would have cost them thousands if they'd cancelled at such a late date, and her partner had to get back to work. She avoided the dark kitchen—the scene of her attack. She had briefly poked her head in the room and glimpsed a spot of blood on the skirting board. Her partner had attempted to clean up, but he'd missed the smear. And a whiff of *his* aftershave lingered in the doorway. She'd swiftly retreated to the safety of the sofa.

The house was deafeningly silent, yet she feared she would hear about another victim like her if she turned on the TV or radio. *Will I ever be able to watch TV again? Will I ever be able to look at my beloved possessions without feeling hatred? Those men touched and searched through everything in my home—will this sense of violation ever fade?* The memory of what had happened that night filled her mind. She shuddered and winced as the pain from her injured leg and arm reacted to her trembling.

Did I lock the front door after Kevin left? Her fear escalated once again. She began hyperventilating then urged herself to inhale and exhale large breaths. Her lungs felt as if they were a raging inferno. She stared at the doorway, envisioning her attacker charging towards her again. She shuffled farther back into the sofa, hoping against hope that it would gobble her up and transport her back to happier times.

She licked her lips, desperate for a drink but too scared to move from the sofa. *Kevin will be home in a couple of hours. He'll make me a drink then.* Night was falling, and headlights from passing cars lit the room through a gap in the velvet curtains. She stood up awkwardly to close the curtains but froze when she spotted him.

In the drizzling rain, standing close to the lamppost on the other side of the road, was a hooded figure looking directly at her. She swiftly closed the curtains, hobbled back from the window and wrapped her arms around herself. Her mobile rang, and she almost shot into the ceiling. Thinking the call was from her partner, she answered it without hesitation. "Kevin, my God! There's a man here. Please come home."

A chilling laugh filled her ear.

Her hand gripped the phone, and a cold chill ran through her body.

"Hello, Maxine."

Confusion lingered. "Kevin, is that you?"

"Call me what you like darling, but don't hang up, or Kevin will get hurt."

Maxine's heart sank. The phone, in her shaking hand, hit the side of her face several times until she gripped it with both hands. The voice was unfamiliar; she didn't recognise it as her attacker's. *Not again! This can't be happening to me again!* Her dry mouth suppressed the scream rising in her throat.

"Wise choice. I like that—a bitch who's prepared to listen," the man growled. "I know you're alone in that lovely house of yours. This is a friendly warning, *Maxine*. Keep your fucking mouth shut. If I catch wind of you chatting with the police again, I'll come and finish you off myself. Got that?"

Maxine's mind shut down. Any kind of response escaped her. The man's chilling laughter filled her ear once more. The phone dropped from her hands, she slumped onto the floor, and everything went black.

CHAPTER TWENTY

Having conversations while standing in the corridor of Scotland Yard was becoming second nature to Angie. She quickly rang home.

"I'm sorry, Warren. I can't talk for long."

"Hello, who is this? It can't be that beautiful wife of mine. She wouldn't neglect to ring me for so long, no matter how much work was piling on top of her."

Angie smiled. Ever the joker, Warren was so forgiving where her work was concerned, unlike other men married to serving women police officers. "I know, and I can't apologise enough."

"Then don't. There's no need."

"How are you and Luke? Are you eating?"

Warren laughed. It was infectious, and Angie joined him. A smile hadn't touched her lips in a while.

"Christ, Angie, you've only been gone one night—"

"And a day!"

"That doesn't count. You're usually at work during the day anyway," he teased.

"Touché! I miss you. Glad you're coping well without me."

"We miss you too. Any developments with your case?"

"Well, the undercover operation has begun. We've got a man on the inside now at least."

"Why do I sense a but coming?"

"I'm not sure. Maybe it's just because I'm tired. I can't seem to stop the self-doubt from kicking in. The team haven't proven anything to me out in the field yet."

"Angie, you're a terrific detective inspector. Your judgement of characters is usually second to none. Give yourself some credit, love. You're surrounded by people who have been hand-picked for this important team. Everyone has their own strengths and weaknesses that will take time to get to know. The more you doubt yourself, the harder that task is going to be, for the whole team. This is a difficult first case for all of you to tackle, but you know what has to be done to save innocent lives."

She recognised the truth in his words. Her confidence returned and brushed aside the doubts. Sometimes she swore he knew her better than she knew herself. His support had often spurred her on to make tough decisions in the past, both in her personal life and throughout her career.

"You're a Godsend. That's just what I needed to hear, Warren."

"There's more to me than just a handsome face, babe."

She could hear the smile in his voice and imagined the adjoining wink. "We're doing all we can to capture these bastards. Hopefully, it won't be long before I'm home."

Warren wolf-whistled, the way he always did when he sensed he was on a promise.

She cupped the phone with her free hand and whispered sexily, "I can't wait to get my hands on you, Mr. North."

"Music to my ears. Now, go and do what you do best, hot stuff. Love you."

"Love you too."

Angie ended the call and took a few deep breaths. Warren could still turn her on even over the phone. Composing herself, she returned to the team.

Angie's colleagues were gathered along the investigation wall at the end of the office. It was rigged with a black sheet that any member of the team could quickly pull down if someone outside the investigation visited the office. Tommy was perched on the end of his desk, his chin resting between his thumb and forefinger. Colin stood beside him; he had the build and demeanour of a bodyguard. Frank sat in the chair closest to the wall, peering up at Jill, who was updating the team on what they had discovered over the past forty-eight hours.

Images of the victims were taped to the wall in a row above those of all the gang members of interest: Duke Mason, Dev Ashward, Chris Strange, Tyler Granger, and Malcom 'Malc' Barry. Coloured pins marked the crime scenes, and a black thread outlined the area where Streetlife was known to operate.

"So, they're the main players." Colin frowned and folded his arms tightly across his chest. "But they're only the tip of this pyramid. This gang will be full of vile creatures we haven't even stumbled across yet. I'd say anything from primary school-aged runners to filthy no-mark pimps."

"That's why this operation is so important." Angie walked towards the group. "Even if we can't secure the names of the entire gang right now, I'm confident reeling in the big fish will make a difference."

"You're right, and if he sings, we could wipe the entire gang off the streets. One less to cope with, out of the dozens parading themselves out there." Colin nodded, his frown slowly dispersing.

"Dozens? I'd put that figure more at hundreds across London," Frank grumbled.

"Ridding the capital of a notorious gang like Streetlife will have two lasting effects. Not only would it benefit the residents who are terrified to step foot outside their own homes, but it would also be a huge accomplishment for us," Angie said, hoping her positivity combatted Frank's sullen words.

"One more thing," Colin added, "it'll probably kick-start another fire under the remaining gangs. They'll be intent on fighting for top position, which may be their downfall now we're on the scene, and create a domino effect to our advantage. We'll be able to put a lot more gangs out of business in the process."

Colin's enthusiasm filled her with pride. His experience working with the Vice Unit was invaluable. If his face hadn't been so well known in London, he would have been the most suitable candidate for the undercover role. *There you go with the doubts again. Stop worrying!*

Breaking out of his contemplative mode, Tommy stood up. "I'm worried that we haven't heard from Scott yet." As if he needed to clarify his concerns he added, "I'm not doubting he's a grand copper. However, it's been almost twenty-four hours, and we've had no word from him. Maybe this has happened all too soon."

Angie could see the cogs turning in Tommy's mind. It was uncanny how his thoughts mirrored her own, but Warren's lingering words of encouragement forced her not to openly admit defeat. As she was about to remind Tommy of the urgency to capture this vile gang, Colin lifted his arms in the air.

"What? You think the boy can just ring us at will?" he shouted, quickly gaining everyone's attention with his uncharacteristic outburst. "The strain of being undercover is immense, guys. Give him a break. Taking on a new persona in the short amount of time he had to prepare for the role is a massive ask for anyone. Add to that he'll be on tenterhooks, hoping against hell that he can pull it off in front of a bunch of dangerous criminals." He folded his arms again and lowered his voice. "How suspicious would it be to Duke and his men if Scott kept making excuses to leave his new group of friends to use his phone?"

"I understand what you're saying, Colin," Jill piped up. "However, we also have to remember Scott's past and his connection with drugs and the gang side of things."

Frank's eyes widened. "Jesus, that's a bit unfair. That was his brother's weakness – an addiction he's trying to help the young boy control. Do you honestly think he's going to put the operation at risk by involving himself with drugs?"

"To be honest, Frank, he might have to," Colin said solemnly as a dark cloud descended over the team. "They don't appreciate newcomers turning up out of the blue. They'll be testing him from the word go. Gang life is not for the faint-hearted. He'll be forced to make tough decisions of his own. He'll need to do what it takes not to get caught. If that includes smoking a joint then that's what he'll have to do."

Jill placed her hands on her hips. "So that makes it okay to partake in illegal and unethical activities?"

"I take it you've never been undercover!" Colin rolled his eyes in frustration.

Jill's stance surprised Angie. While the debate was an interesting one, she could feel the team's individual tempers rising. They had been around each other non-stop for forty-eight hours, away from their loved ones, and their crankiness was beginning to show. She needed to step in before things escalated further and someone said something they would later regret.

"Stop! This is getting us nowhere," she said. "What's the point deliberating the ifs, buts, and maybes? A few days ago, we all sat around that table and agreed this was the only way forward for this case and that Scott was the officer to put his life on the line and go undercover. What's done is done; we need to live by our decisions. I take on board everything you're saying, but I'm inclined to agree with Colin. Scott is in this up to his neck. We should trust that he'll do everything he can to get in contact with us. It's a waiting game for now."

Jill nodded. "You're right, Angie. I apologise for my outburst. I think we're all a bit tense at the moment, and worried about Scott's safety." She dropped wearily into the chair.

Angie scanned the room. *Am I pushing them too hard?* She could see the tiredness in everyone's eyes but had a feeling if she suggested they all go home for a rest, her colleagues would bite her head off. Their passion had just portrayed their determination to help Scott apprehend this gang.

"Right, I say we put a secondary plan in motion," Tommy suggested, sounding uncertain. "Perhaps we could send a bogus pizza delivery to Mason's home. Maybe someone could assess the situation from that angle?"

Angie's mind buzzed at the thought. With the constant flow of people in and out of Duke Mason's flat, she had no idea if Scott was still there, or whether he was even still alive, for that matter. The pinging noise of a text message notification interrupted her worrying. A message had finally arrived on the team's mobile.

Tommy snatched the phone off the desk and read the message. "Scott's finally got in touch. Maxine Dyer's in danger."

CHAPTER TWENTY-ONE

Angie gripped the handle on the car door as they pulled up outside Maxine Dyer's home. She turned to look at Tommy and Frank. The taunting image of the bruised and battered woman lying in the hospital bed flashed before her. "Are you guys ready for this?"

The two men nodded and said in unison, "Let's do it."

Scott's tiny message, four simple words, had filled Angie with dread and confusion. She rang the hospital, and they'd confirmed that Maxine had discharged herself. To learn that she was back home and in danger had shocked Angie to her core. She was desperate to enter the house and rescue the poor woman, *if* she was still alive. So many questions were dashing through her mind: *Why did she discharge herself? Did Dr. Sammoutis try to prevent her from leaving? Was anyone at home protecting her?* But the major question was why the uniformed police officer guarding her room had neglected to inform the team of the latest development. She made a mental note to pull the officer over the coals for his unprofessionalism.

"Hold on, boss," Tommy mumbled, before either of them had the chance to get out of the car. "The front door's ajar."

She quickly surveyed the area. "By the looks of it, there's no access to the rear of the property. Frank, call for uniform backup and then wait for them out here. If you see anyone leave the property, pounce on them. Don't let them get away."

"Yes, boss!"

"Tommy, come with me."

Angie bolted from the car. They sprinted across the road and stopped abruptly outside Maxine's front door. The pair strained to see through the gap in the door. Murmurings came from inside. Unable to ascertain what was being said or who the voices belonged to, she called out, "This is Detective Inspector Angie North! Maxine, can you hear me?"

She pushed open the door, but an enormous bald man filled the doorway, tattoos down the length of his arms. Angie gulped, then Tommy swept her aside, blocking the man's path.

"We're from Scotland Yard. Identify yourself," Tommy demanded, totally in charge of the situation.

"About fucking time!" the man's bewildered look disappeared. "Get in here and help her," the man pleaded, his shoulders slouching as he stepped aside, allowing them to enter.

Angie wasn't about to let this man dupe her into a false sense of security. "I'm Detective Inspector Angie North. Identify yourself." She pulled her warrant card from her jacket pocket and thrust it in the man's face.

"What the fuck? This is my house! Aren't you here to help Maxine?"

"Are you Kevin? Did you call the police, sir?" Tommy asked.

"I am. No! I assumed Maxine did before she fainted."

Angie's patience was wearing thin. If Maxine Dyer really was lying unconscious somewhere in the house, they needed to get to her fast. "Have you called an ambulance?"

The man shook his head. "No, I just got here. She's awake now; she says she's okay."

"Tommy, call Frank and take this man into the kitchen, confirm his identity."

"Boss—"

Angie barged past the stranger and marched up the hallway. She could hear muffled groans as Tommy escorted the man through the house. Any worries about walking into a trap disappeared as soon as she saw Maxine Dyer curled in the foetal position on the sofa. The woman's head rocked from side to side. Since she'd last laid eyes on Maxine, the bruises had intensified in colour. Subtle purples had turned into deep-mauve, almost black, patches on her face. Her eyes appeared to be even more swollen. Her other injuries were disguised by her loose-fitting clothing, however there was no doubting the fear exuding from every pore of her small frame.

"Maxine, do you remember me? I'm Detective Inspector Angie North. I visited you at the hospital a few days ago."

Maxine rocked faster, as if Angie's words had triggered something in her mind. Angie looked around the room. Nothing appeared to be disturbed.

"No... no... no," Maxine whispered.

Angie sat on the edge of the sofa and gently placed her hand on top of the woman's. "Can you tell me what happened, Maxine? Has someone been in your house?"

"Get out!" she suddenly screamed, yanking her hand away.

"I'm not going anywhere until you tell me what's wrong."

"You have to leave!" Maxine yelled again.

The man she'd met at the door stormed into the room and hugged Maxine. Angie left the sofa and stared at Tommy standing in the doorway.

He nodded. "His story checks out, boss. This is Kevin Salter—Maxine's partner. He lives here too. Uniforms have just arrived and Frank's gone to meet them."

"Tell them to hold off." Angie raised her hand and turned back to the couple entwined on the sofa.

"What did you say to upset her?" Kevin growled.

"Mr. Salter, I'm trying to ascertain why Maxine is so frightened."

"I don't know!" Kevin tightened his hold on Maxine but looked Angie in the eye. "I had to go to work. I thought Maxine would be all right for a few hours, with the doors locked. I promised to check in as often as I could. I called her for half an hour… she didn't answer. I panicked and rushed back here."

"Did someone break into your home, Maxine?" Angie tried again.

"I don't think so," Kevin answered instead of Maxine. "The door was locked when I arrived. She was lying on the floor, just staring into space like a nut job."

"Shh! Don't tell them anything else," Maxine whispered, her eyes darting around the room.

"Why not, darling?" Kevin loosened his grip and placed his hand under her chin, forcing her to look at him.

Maxine swiftly turned her head, escaping his grasp. Her body swayed violently. "He'll kill me."

Kevin frowned, and Angie noticed his clenched fists. She followed the woman's eyes to the floor and noticed a mobile phone poking out from under the coffee table. Angie bent down to retrieve it.

"You have to fucking help her! She can't live like this, with those scumbags out there, taunting her. If I find the bastard who's done this… who laid his paws on—"

"Calm down, Mr. Salter," Tommy said, re-entering the room.

"Fucking calm down? Look at her." Kevin rested his head on Maxine's shoulder.

Angie turned to her partner. "I'm going to assume Miss. Dyer received a phone call from her attacker."

"He called again?" Kevin asked.

"The front door was locked, and there's no obvious sign of disturbance. I've been watching her. Her eyes have been drawn to that phone—"

"She should be in witness protection," Kevin demanded.

"That's a tough call. We can offer police protection only at this time. Tommy, get uniform to escort Maxine and Mr. Salter to the station."

Angie's mind began churning. She studied Maxine, watching the tears silently running down her bruised face.

"What are you thinking, boss?" Tommy asked.

She led Tommy by the elbow out of the room. "Something's wrong. Maxine was being guarded by a uniformed officer at the hospital. Tell me how she managed to discharge herself. How is it we didn't hear she was at home and yet her attacker found out?" Angie's cheeks warmed as her temper rose. "Someone has messed up big time. Not one of our team—someone at the hospital—and that person has just put Maxine's life in danger, again!"

"I'm with you. What a cock-up, boss! Maybe Jill will have some news for us on that front when we get back.

It's a blessing Maxine wasn't confronted by this man in person and only received a phone call."

She contemplated the situation. "Or perhaps the boyfriend's arrival saved her? Either way, this shouldn't have occurred."

Angie left the house. The cold night breeze was a welcome relief on her fiery cheeks. She and Tommy made their way over to where Frank and the uniformed officers were waiting at the end of the path. Angie discussed what needed to be done next. She followed Tommy to the car, thinking of her undercover officer's safety.

CHAPTER TWENTY-TWO

After a full morning of suspect profiling, cross checking and implementing plans, Angie and Tommy sat in a snug corner of the White Horse public house. She had strategically placed her hand over his on the table. Her other, lightly gripped the stem of a wine glass. They sat with their faces close, pretending to be lovers in deep conversation while waiting for Scott.

The White Horse was exceptionally busy, despite it being midweek and just after noon. Groups of women were chatting over lunch, and men were shouting at the rerun of a football game on the large-screen TV. Angie and Tommy integrated well as just another couple enjoying each other's company. The pub was situated on Brixton Hill, sandwiched between the shops on the high street and within walking distance of Brixton's underground station. Tommy had sent Scott a text message the night before instructing him to meet them at the pub at twelve thirty.

Angie angled her chair and eyed the door. She released Tommy's hand and lifted her wine glass, the anxiety mounting in her gut. Scott hadn't replied to the text, and she wondered if it was time to move in and pull him out. Sipping her drink, she spotted Scott waltz into the bar, his black leather jacket and jeans making him look younger than his twenty-eight years.

Tommy casually nodded at Scott, who stopped at the bar and bought himself a pint of beer before joining them. Angie had a feeling that Scott's chilled expression meant he was about to tell them he'd been successful. Either that, or he was a damn good actor.

Scott shook Tommy's outstretched hand as if they were old friends. Angie peered over his shoulder, to see if he'd been followed. He hadn't.

Tommy leaned in, his voice low, "How are you, mate?"

"Tired," he replied.

Angie noticed Scott's bloodshot eyes. "We weren't sure you received our message, when you didn't reply."

"They do everything together in this gang." Scott paused and gulped down a large mouthful of beer. "Duke's been watching me like a hawk, sizing me up."

"You think he's sussed you out?" Angie asked.

"No, but I think he's being super cautious."

"Was it difficult to get away?"

"He wants to know the ins and outs of everything. I had to bide my time, leave when Chris did. It was the only way. We'd made the excuse we needed to change our clothes. I've told him to take a walk. He's meeting me back here in twenty minutes."

"Okay, let's keep this brief then," Angie said. "Tell us what you know?"

"I've got most of the details from Billy, one of Duke's guys. He's pretty keen to chat. Tyler and Malc are definitely our attackers. They've committed all the murders. They're new to the area, and to Streetlife, and although Duke didn't instigate the attacks, he's still supplying them with the phone numbers for their scam. Dev—he's Duke's right-hand man and the guy from Frank's photo—is a computer genius. He hacked into a local phone company's records and is pulling all the names and numbers of women in the area who have taken out a contract mobile phone with that company." Scott drained more of his pint. "The scam involves calling the women, with the intention of finding out when they'll be away from the house, and breaking in. Only Tyler and Malc seem to be making a point of showing up when these women are at home."

"We need to move in, quick," Angie said eagerly. "Surely we have enough evidence now to nail Tyler and Malc, and with you on the inside, we can tie Duke and his other cronies to the scam too. Is that achievable, Scott?"

"Duke is definitely starting to trust me. He's talking more freely in front of me. He's guarded, though, keen not to mention specifics in my presence, but I think it's doable." Scott nodded. "He called Maxine, to put the frighteners on her. Is she okay?"

"Shaken up, as you can imagine. We got your message and rushed over there. We assumed he had visited her in person. She passed out at her house; her boyfriend found her before we got there."

"He was planning on going around there to see her. He was high on booze and drugs. I suggested he phone her instead. He sent one of his boys, Billy—I don't know his surname yet—just to keep an eye on her address while he made the call." Scott hung his head in shame. "Sorry if I did the wrong thing, boss. The woman must've been scared shitless. I couldn't get any time on my own, or I would've sent the text sooner."

"You did the right thing. It was a difficult situation." Angie smiled, appeased by his explanation. "If Duke had gone to the house, she might not be with us now. I've put her under police protection."

Scott sighed heavily, looking ashamed. Angie worried that his undercover actions were weighing him down.

"How did they know Maxine was at home?" Angie asked, eager to get their meeting back on track.

"Dev knows a nurse on the ward. She, shall we say, *distracted* the uniformed officer while Maxine arranged her release. She lifted the home address from the discharge papers and sent them to Dev."

"That's certainly different to what the officer told Jill, so we'll be pulling him in again. As for the nurse, she'll be going down as an accessory in all of this." Angie was disgusted by the nurse's betrayal. Nurses were supposed to be professional, compassionate and honest people. Her blood boiled. The gang clearly had contacts everywhere.

"Right," Angie said while Scott finished his beer. "When we get back to the office, we'll be putting the sting operation in motion. Scott, I need you to be ready. Gain Duke's trust, but don't let that phone out of your sight. We'll be in touch in the next twenty-four hours with our plan."

"Hear you loud and clear." Scott saluted her. He rose from his chair without saying another word, shook Tommy's hand once again, and exited the pub.

"Let's move!" she said once Scott was out of sight.

The team spent the next few hours devising strategies, consulting SCO19, and preparing their attack on the Streetlife gang. Before confirming their plans with the DCI, Angie ran through everything one final time. This was the team's chance to raise any doubts. Everyone agreed the plan was a good one and that their priority should be to get Scott out of the gang's clutches without them smelling a rat.

"How did he seem to you?" Jill enquired.

"Exhausted. Although he was pretty sure he's made a good impression with Mason." Angie paused, then added, "Just to recap, a property in Lambeth North has been secured. That's where we'll entice Duke and his crew. Jill is going to pose as the homeowner. Colin and Frank, you'll be positioned upstairs, in close enough proximity should Jill need any assistance. Tommy and I will secure the perimeter with SCO19, out of sight, using the surrounding houses and gardens as cover. Now, Lambeth is only fifteen to twenty minutes from Brixton station by car, so it's within their limit. Scott will propose they up their game and approach a more affluent area."

"What will Todd's cover story be?" Jill asked.

"Todd's mother is a cleaner and works in various houses in the area. Todd has visited these properties and knows the valuables they contain. He'll also know a few of the homes will be empty, as the homeowners are on holiday, and hint about a hidden safe, paintings and jewellery that he's seen."

"So, if they're expecting the house to be empty, what excuse is Jill going to come up with for being at home?" Frank asked, looking confused.

"If Duke or his men ask why Jill is at home, she'll tell them her holiday was cancelled due to her husband having to work. There's no need for concern. The area will be completely surrounded. We'll move in and arrest them before they can go on the offensive."

Angie glanced at Jill, searching her colleague's expression, but the woman never faltered. She was poised with the next question. "Can we ensure more than one gang member will be present?"

"That'll be down to Scott. Let's hope he can pull it off. It's a bigger house than the previous ones they've hit. A driver will be needed because of the loot on offer."

"How are we getting this information to Scott?" Jill asked.

"Tommy has sent Scott a message, told him to meet at the White Horse again at nine this evening."

"Boss, I hope you don't mind me saying… I think it should be me who meets Scott at the pub tonight," Colin said, a hint of trepidation in his voice.

Angie frowned. "Why?"

"The three of you have already met there once today. It might look a bit suspicious to the locals and perhaps one of Duke's snitches if Scott meets up with Tommy twice in the same day."

"Hmm… you could be right! I have to say, I like the way your mind works, Colin."

He blushed slightly, and Angie suppressed a chuckle for embarrassing him in front of the team.

"I know you're concerned about my previous role in Vice, but I was based more in central London—and sadly, I've lost some hair and put on a few pounds since those days." Colin's joke lightened the mood in the room.

Angie warmed to Colin the more time she spent with him. He was a level-headed player who would take calculated risks out in the field without putting a colleague in harm's way. He had a style about him that she was drawn to—the joker who oozed common sense.

"That's decided then." Angie clicked her fingers. "In a few hours, Colin will meet Scott and instruct him about tomorrow night's sting operation."

CHAPTER TWENTY-THREE

Scott waited in the pub, nursing his second pint of the day. He intended to savour this one, instead of necking it quickly. He'd found it much easier to get away from the gang this evening as Duke and Dev had their own plans, which they were keen to keep close to their chests. Scott had yet to decide if Duke trusted him. During their drug fest, he'd appeared to treat him like an old friend, but when the fuzziness lifted from Duke's mind, he'd become more guarded. Perhaps the drugs had influenced his mood swings, or maybe Duke was playing mind games as a way of testing him.

He shook his head, plagued by the out-of-character choices he'd been forced to make over the past few days. Naively, he hadn't anticipated that he would be expected to take any form of drugs. He ran his fingers through his hair, suddenly feeling dirty, contaminated, and ashamed. His left leg twitched nervously as if it had a life of its own, and a desire to get back to normality surged through him.

"All right, mate!"

He turned, his leg now still, to see Colin smiling down at him. His colleague sat opposite him, and he felt relieved Angie hadn't shown up instead.

"Shit! You're as white as a ghost. Didn't mean to spook you."

Scott's hand swept over his face and down his neck. He was desperate for a shower. "Sleep has kind of evaded me over the last few days."

"I understand. You finding it tougher than you thought it was going to be?"

"I have to admit I am. One good thing has come out of this, though."

Colin cocked his head a little. "What's that?"

"It has made me even more determined to get Ross off the drugs."

Colin nodded and took a sip from his pint. "I can understand that, mate. It won't be easy if he's been on them for years. You'll have to lock him away somewhere, let him go cold turkey, unless you've got the funds to put him in one of those fancy rehabilitation centres."

"I haven't, unfortunately. Guess I'll keep buying a lottery ticket every week instead." Eager to get off the subject, he asked, "So, what's the plan?" His nerves struck up, and his leg began to judder again.

Colin spent the next ten minutes informing him about the team's plan. Scott listened carefully, sipped his beer, and nodded now and again, but didn't interrupt. He was too busy working out the pressure it would put him under when he returned to the gang. Colin relayed the information without hesitation, which in turn filled Scott with confidence that the team had worked hard to formulate the plan. He was grateful the team had come up with a secure operation. *I knew they wouldn't let me down.* Hearing the words *sting*, *SCO19* and *arrest* sparked his officer's brain into action as he began to make plans of his own for getting Duke to go along with the scheme.

"Well? What do you think?" Colin took a large gulp from his glass.

Scott leaned forward. "It could work, providing I can hook Duke with the idea."

"Glad you think so. Our main concern is the fact that Duke himself has never been involved in the crimes against the women victims. Can you be sure he'll want to be included personally in this?"

"Duke's already mentioned the phone scam to me in passing. I intentionally didn't show much interest at the time, just in case he was testing me. Since I've been there, neither Tyler nor Malc have visited the flat. Not sure why. Maybe they go off to do their own thing now and then. I suppose I could suggest partnering Chris on a break-in. But hopefully his greed will come into play once I explain this job could keep him comfortable for months, at least. I'll be overexcited about it and suggest we should double up, hit the area with two teams instead of one. Depends how greedy he is or whether Dev sees through the plan and tries to dissuade him. Dev's definitely the brains in this gang. He pulls Duke's strings a lot of the time. Although I think Duke's need for power will be the defining factor in the end."

"Sounds like you have every one of them sussed already, mate. I'm glad. It's weird the ones we're after have gone AWOL though, don't you think?"

"Are Tyler and Malc still under surveillance?"

"Not as such, but we have tabs on their whereabouts." Colin paused when Scott exhaled a deep breath. "You sure everything is okay, mate?"

Scott held up his hand in front of him and waved it from side to side. "Yes and no. Well…" He was unsure whether to share his doubts with Colin, fearing it would make him come across as a wuss.

An understanding smile pulled at Colin's lips. "You're bound to be dubious, mate. It's your first undercover operation. I bet everyone has to tackle that internal battle of what is right and wrong at times like this when they're pretending to be someone they're not."

"You hit the nail on the head! These guys will likely string me up if they find out who I am. Maybe that's why they keep supplying me with drugs—to see if I'll slip up."

"You're probably right. I've been there, sometimes for months at a time. It was my decision to come and meet you tonight. I wanted to stress how important this sting operation is. You've been with them forty-eight hours now, and they haven't sussed you yet. You're doing a great job, Scott. Keep doing what feels right in the situation, and we'll get the bastards."

"I'll do my best to string them along for a little longer."

"You do that, mate. You'll be out of there by tomorrow night."

He found Colin's words reassuring, and a huge weight lifted from his shoulders. He would be able to cope with the strain for another forty-eight hours or so.

"Let's have another pint. You can go over your story with me before you head back and sell it to Duke. Recapping it a few more times will make it seem more real rather than just a plan that's been flung together at the last minute."

After downing another beer and slotting all the pieces of the operation together, Scott left the pub. It was almost ten o'clock and the night sky was clear. He was torn between returning to Duke's flat or going to Chris's dive. He decided to bite the bullet and head back to Duke's. Maybe the whole gang would be there—and that could work in his favour. If his proposal aroused interest from the others, Duke might give the plan more thought. Scott strolled along Brixton Hill, the cold air sobering his two-pint haze. Colin's words of wisdom had restored his confidence that he was indeed the best man for the task in hand.

Scott approached the estate, where the smell of marijuana hung heavily in the fresh night air. The children's play area, if it could be called that after all the equipment had been yanked from the concrete, was filled with loud voices and hysterical laughter. He strained his eyes. In the dimly lit playground, flickering streetlights revealed the outlines of at least ten youths. His heart pounded. He didn't have a good feeling about what lay ahead.

He pulled up the collar of his jacket, clenched his fists down by his side, and marched towards them. He had no idea who they were. He presumed they belonged to a rival gang, setting out to test Duke's patience by lingering on his patch.

The youths fell silent as Scott drew closer. Breaking into a run crossed his mind, but his inner voice warned him how reckless that would be. He decided to play it cool.

"Who the fuck's that?" a voice bellowed from about ten feet away.

"Don't let him sneak past. Grab him!" a different youth shouted.

Scott froze as the dark figures moved closer. Their laughter struck up again, this time with a menacing echo. Five of the youths jumped the rickety fence surrounding the play area and blocked his path. The others remained in the distance, egging their friends on. The five hooded figures circled him like a pack of wolves.

"What's up, guys?" Scott asked, pushing down the fear.

The group closed in tighter, forming a circle around him. They mumbled to each other, and one youth jabbed Scott in the ribs. He didn't retaliate, fearing one of them would try to slice his throat with a blade or put a bullet in his head. He still hadn't learned what weapons were carried on the estate. They edged in, suffocating him, and just as he was about to lash out, he heard a familiar voice.

"Hey! Leave off. That's my cuz you're messing with."

Scott sighed with relief as he fought against the dizziness. Chris Strange, his unexpected saviour, stepped out of the shadows and stood beside him. Scott felt the youths' disappointment as they retreated back into the park to join the rest of the group. He nodded at Chris, grateful for his intervention.

Chris leaned in close. "Bit fucking stupid walking through here on your own, man."

"I didn't think. Cheers for that."

"Whatever."

"Where are Duke and Dev? I need a word."

"Is this shit ending soon? I'm feeling fuckin' para. Every time Duke turns my way, I think he's gonna deck me." Chris peered over his shoulder at the group of lads.

Scott thumped him on the top of the arm. "Not here, man. We could be overheard."

"Chill, man. I know these guys. They're—"

"You don't know shit. We need to keep safe," Scott snarled. "Let's get to Duke's. Follow my lead. Got that?"

"Got it! Billy, Fish! We're heading up. You coming?" he called out.

Scott had never met Fish before and made a mental note to tap Chris for information when they were back at the boy's dive of a home. Right then, however, he had one thing on his mind—to get Duke excited about a robbery.

When Scott and Chris reached Duke's flat they heard shouting coming from inside.

"Shit! What's going on?" Scott sensed trouble, which could put his plan in jeopardy.

Chris cursed under his breath. "Sounds like Tyler to me. You ain't had the privilege of meeting these guys yet. Now's your chance." He pounded on the door.

Scott's stomach twisted into knots while they waited for the door to open. *Play it cool! One step out of place, and they'll be down on you!*

Dev yanked open the door. Looking relieved to see them, he grabbed the front of Chris's T-shirt and hauled him in. "You guys better get in there fast before Duke thumps him to the floor."

The three of them rushed through the hallway and barged into the living room. Duke and Tyler were nose to nose, both breathing heavily, imitating raging bulls. Scott held back, determined that the other gang members should be the ones to break up the sparring men.

Chris glared at Malc, who was watching his mate and the gang leader from a distance, his arms folded, as though he didn't give a damn if either of them started a fight.

"Call him off, dickhead," Chris said, "There's only gonna be one winner if they do battle."

Malc shook his head. "I ain't no one's babysitter, man. They've got a problem with each other, and it needs sortin'. You'll keep out of it if you know what's best for ya."

As the heated argument continued, Duke and Tyler were oblivious to what was going on around them. Scott found himself in an invidious position: damned if he got involved, and damned if he didn't. He stepped forward, placing himself in harm's way in between the tall men.

Their chests puffed out, neither of them had any intention of backing down anytime soon.

"Shit, guys. Let's discuss this calmly. We're supposed to be on the same side, ain't we?"

"Out the way, tosser! Who the fuck are you anyway?" Tyler sneered, his eyes darting Scott's way for a split second before returning to Duke.

Duke's lip curled up. "Leave him alone. He's cool. He don't give me grief like you do."

"Fuck off, man. What grief have I given you? All Malc and I are guilty of is supplying you with a load of cash and a ton of jewellery to fence. What's the others brought your way, huh? Fuckin' zilch. They're a bunch of no-marks, takin' you for a fuckin' ride."

"You think you're so fuckin' smart, don't ya? At least the others do as they're instructed on a job."

"Meaning what?" Tyler challenged, a smirk creasing the side of his mouth.

Duke shook his head. "I'm warning you, loser, don't mess with me."

Scott edged farther between the men. "Guys, come on. This is getting too heated. Let's sit down and discuss it properly, lay all our cards on the table and decide what to go to next, eh? Something has cropped up that'll spark both your interests."

Duke turned to look at him. "Now what the fuck are you talking about? Don't you start throwing your fuckin' screwball ideas around, bringing trouble to my door like this gobshite has."

"You're crazy, man. I ain't done *no* such thing," Tyler objected.

"Gentlemen, just give me ten minutes. If you don't like what I have to say, I'll take my proposition elsewhere and leave you two to rip shreds out of each other, okay?"

Duke eyed him with disdain. "Is this some kind of wind-up?"

"No, I swear. The job I've got in mind is gonna set you up in dope for years to come, man, I promise. Just hear me out, yeah?"

"What's in it for Malc and me if we get involved?" Tyler demanded, his chest expanding farther than before.

"That's up to Duke. Shit, man, just let me have the chance to tell you 'bout the scheme first, okay? I'm thinking this is gonna need all of us on board. It ain't gonna be a two- or four-man job, and it's gonna take balls to pull it off. My question to you guys is: do you have what it takes to tackle such a big job?"

Duke stepped back and ran a hand through his hair. "Why ain't you mentioned this before?"

"Would you? If you'd just teamed up with a bunch of strangers? Nah, I didn't think so. This trust has to be a two-way thing, Duke. I've seen enough over the past few days to know where your loyalties lie, to know that I can trust you one hundred percent. I ain't got a clue why you guys are squaring up like this, but if you're showing that much anger, then I think you're pointing it in the wrong direction. What's the deal anyway? Is someone gonna tell me what this shit is all about?"

Duke took his seat next to Dev on the sofa, and Tyler walked across the room to where Malc was leaning against the wall.

After a few seconds, Tyler finally spoke. "All I know is that we had an arrangement and Duke fitted me and Malc up with duff information."

Duke lifted his head back and laughed. "I did?"

"You know it's the truth, man. Fuckin' admit it!"

Scott could sense the tension rising between the men once more. "Why are you still around here then?" he challenged Tyler, thinking as a gang member but sounding like a copper as the words slipped out. He cleared his throat and clarified himself. "I mean, if someone fitted me up, they'd only get one chance to do that. I wouldn't step foot in their gaff again. Yet here you are. Why?"

Tyler hitched up his right shoulder. "He owes me. And I'm here to collect what's owin' to me, to us."

"Have you got a say in this?" Scott aimed his question at Malc.

"I do what Tyler says. We've been together years. He's never done wrong by me."

"What'cha saying, fool? That *I* have?" Duke confronted the quieter man.

"The facts are there as clear as day, man. You screwed with us. What 'ave we ever done to make you wanna do that to us, Duke?" Malc demanded, his voice even and calm.

Duke threw his arms up in the air. "You've gotta be kiddin' me! How fuckin' thick d'ya think I am? The only time any of my boys takes a life is when another gang steps foot on my territory. What you did to those women was fuckin' shameful."

Tyler looked shocked by the revelation.

"What? Did you think I wouldn't find out? The police know—it was on the goddamn TV, dickheads. If you think I want any part of that shit, you're wrong. Jesus, Leroy would be spinning in his grave if he knew this crap had gone down."

"If you didn't appreciate all the tat we hauled from them hits, then you should've spoken out, man, rejected the gear when we emptied it out on the table, but you didn't. Why's that?"

"Ya think I would've accepted the trash if I'd known you'd killed the women, or left one of them for dead."

Tyler frowned. "What'cha talking about?"

Duke shook his head in disgust and brought Dev into the conversation. "He don't know. Shows what a fuckin' loser he is. You tell him, man, 'cause I ain't got the fuckin' patience for this shit no more."

Tyler held up his hand and curled his fingers towards him. "Give it to me, Dev?"

"One of the jobs you done, you left the bitch alive. Now that wench has gone to the police. That's what Duke is getting at. You're going to lead the police to our door—and for what? A few measly grand and some gear that didn't bring in what was expected. Was it fuckin' worth it?"

"Hey, we had no idea about the one still alive. No problem, I'll go round there and finish her off."

Duke sighed heavily and glared at him. "You'll fuckin' leave her alone. You've fucked up enough, man. You leave her for me to deal with. As for the others, well... why? We told ya to hit the places when they were empty. You, in your twisted fuckin' wisdom, thought your way would be better, didn't ya? You make me sick, man. I want you out of this gang, now!"

Scott hesitated before he jumped in with his proposal. "Not so fast, Duke. I understand you feel betrayed, man, but what I have up my sleeve will need *all* of our skills to pull off."

"I don't need any more shit comin' my way, Todd. If this job you're trying to dangle is hot, then why don't ya have a pop at it yourself? My trusting days for newcomers are over." He sliced his hand across his throat to emphasise his point.

Shit! Not what I wanted to hear. Maybe a little kidology will change his mind. He gave a nonchalant shrug. "Whatever! If that's what you want, I won't try and dissuade you otherwise." He turned to walk out the room. "Nice knowin' y'all. I'll see if another gang is willin' to hear me out on this job. Catch ya later, Chris, back at the flat."

"Wait! Spill the beans on what's on offer, and then I'll decide if I want it or out," Duke shouted.

Scott spun around to face the gang again. He pointed to his chest. "Wait a minute—you think I'm stupid, or what? You want me to hand over all the information without knowing if you want to go through with the hit or not? What kind of fool are you takin' me for, man? There's a trust issue here, and the problem ain't on my side of the fence." His nerves jangled harder. He clenched and unclenched his fists as if he were playing with the red stress toy he kept in his office drawer.

"I dunno, man. I've told you! This shit with these two clowns has dented my trust."

"And the words 'this hit will set you up in drugs and money for life' didn't have an impact?"

"Maybe it tempted me a little. Damaged trust is a lot to swallow, man."

"I appreciate that, Duke, but I ain't the one who damaged your trust, am I?"

Duke looked at Dev. "Well, what d'ya think? Does it sound like something we should be interested in?"

Dev tutted. "Let's hear what the guy has to say. We've got no reason not to trust him, but don't forget he's Chris's cousin. If there were any doubts about him, Chris wouldn't have brought him into the fold. That right, Chris?"

Everyone turned to gaze at Chris. He shuffled his feet, and Scott had a feeling the youngster was about to crumble under the pressure.

Scott spoke up before Chris had a chance to answer. "Shit, you guys really are a class act. What's with doubting Chris all of a sudden? What's he done to deserve this shit, Duke? Hey, I have my answer right there—I'm outta here. I'll have no trouble attracting the right team to go in with me on this one, not when I tell them what's on offer."

Chris held his hands in front of him. "I know what's on offer, and you need to listen up, Duke. Todd ain't pulling a fast one, not like Tyler." He turned and snarled at Tyler. "I never liked you from the minute you stepped in here, you fuckin' nutcase!"

Tyler marched across the room and grabbed Chris round the throat. "You what? You crippling waste of space! 'Yes, no boy,' that's what we call you 'cause that's all you ever say. What the fuck do you bring to the table, eh? Nothing! Yet here you are, dissing me. Get a fuckin' life, shit for brains."

Scott jumped in to defend his make-believe cousin. "Cut it out. Stop pointing the finger in someone else's direction when you're to blame for all the fuckin' tension around here."

"He's right—back off. Chris ain't done nothing wrong. You say we need these clowns in on the act if we're going to pull this hit off, Todd?" Duke asked, motioning with his head first to Tyler and then Malc, as Tyler released his grip on Chris.

Scott nodded. "Yep, it's a big one. All hands on deck an' all that."

"Why don't we give them one final chance, Duke? They ain't gonna be stupid again after us finding out what they've been up to." Dev turned to Tyler. "Are you?"

"You've got our word. We want a decent share of the grab, though."

Duke laughed. "You've got a fuckin' nerve, I'll give you that. I'm willing to take another risk just for this job."

Scott released his breath through a gap in his lips. "Good. Listen up—this is the hit…"

CHAPTER TWENTY-FOUR

Angie and the team spent the day going over the case from the beginning, to ensure they hadn't missed anything that would likely jeopardise the sting operation. She'd never asked a female officer to put her life in danger before, which irritated her. Still, if she and her female colleagues insisted on being taken seriously by their male colleagues, it was a necessary undertaking.

This plan was top-heavy with risks. In one way, she was intrigued to see how her troops responded in a crisis. However, on the flip side of that coin, she found herself envying Jill. When she was just starting out in the force, and her priority was to impress her male colleagues, she wouldn't have hesitated to put herself forward for Jill's role in the operations. Nowadays, most of her DI duties seemed to involve the delegation of such dangerous roles. Maybe she could have a word with Channing about that side of things once the current operation was over. That was not to say that she didn't have confidence in Jill— she did—and Jill wouldn't be out of the team's sight anyway, not with SCO19 on hand at the location. Their backup, she hoped, would put everyone's mind at ease.

Inspector Davies, the duty inspector of the SCO19 team deployed for the operation, was in constant contact with Angie. Everyone involved in the case understood how costly a slip-up could be to the two undercover officers involved. Since the plan had been formulated and during their conversations, Inspector Davies had assured Angie that no unnecessary gunfire would take place unless either officer's life was in grave danger. It was agreed, after Scott had informed them that he didn't anticipate any weapons being used by the gang, that each of the SCO19 team members would have their usual weapons at the ready. Scott was going to try to dissuade the gang if the situation changed.

Angie stopped by Jill's desk and perched on the edge. "How are you feeling?"

"Actually, not too bad. I thought I'd be more nervous than I am. That's bound to change once I get in the house, I suppose. What about you? What with this being your first major operation in charge, at least on this team?"

"The same as you. I'm okay at the moment, but who's to say how we're going to feel tomorrow? Have you got anything special planned for this evening with hubby?"

"What, in case I don't make it out of there alive?" Jill laughed.

"Crap, that's not what I meant. Sorry if that's how it sounded."

"It didn't. I just wanted to see your reaction."

Angie swiped the top of Jill's arm. "Hey, don't you start! I thought the men on this team were bad enough at winding me up."

"Sorry. No, I haven't got anything special planned, just an early night. What's the betting I don't get any sleep?"

"I don't know what else I can say to reassure you, except that it's my reputation as a DI on the line here, so you'd better believe that neither me, nor the team, will screw up. How's that?"

Jill smiled. "Nice try, boss."

"Okay, I want you to take off early today. I've already cleared it with Channing."

"There's no need for that. I'll do my share around here and knock off at the normal time. Actually, I'd rather do that than sit around at home, dwelling on what's expected of me tomorrow."

"That's exactly how I'd feel if I were in your shoes. All right, I'll leave the decision up to you. If you fancy taking off, just do it, okay?"

"I appreciate that. Thank you."

She moved on to Colin. "Everything all right?"

He looked up from his computer screen. "Yes, boss. Shouldn't it be?"

"Just checking. I wanted to ask how you thought Scott was holding up last night when you met up with him."

"Honestly? He seemed really calm to me. We had time for a couple of beers, during which there were a few instances when he went quiet. Who could blame him there, right?"

"Quiet? Do you think he's regretting going undercover?"

"I'm not sure. Anyway, he sent me a text a few hours after we went our separate ways, said that everything had gone according to plan and that Duke and his men were hooked on the idea."

"Was there any doubt about that? Given the gang's penchant for burglary?"

"He said there was a moment when he almost walked away from Duke's place."

"He did well to keep the gang's interest then. Okay, we'll put the final details in place around four this afternoon before we call it a day."

"I think everyone is sure of their roles by now, boss."

"It won't hurt to go over it one last ti—" The phone rang on her desk. "Hello, DI North speaking."

"It's DCI Channing. Just checking how things are progressing, Inspector. Is everything in hand now? Are all departments, this one and the ones accompanying us on this mission, up to speed on what's expected of them?"

"Yes, sir. My team and I are going over things one final time before we knock off tonight. After that, it'll be down to Scott and Jill to pull this off and bring these bastards down."

"Good, good. I was hoping to drop by and see you later this afternoon, but the Commissioner has requested all the DCIs in the area to join him in his office at three."

"That sounds ominous, sir."

"It does. It happens now and again; he likes to keep us on our toes. Prefers to skip the ranks below him and come down heavy on us directly when the need arises. I fear this is one such occasion, given the tone of his e-mail request."

"Ah, I see. Go direct to the officers on the street to keep everyone else in line, eh?"

"In a roundabout way, yes. Therefore, if he comes down heavy on me, expect a similar result on you and your team."

She winced and replied hesitantly, "Oh, okay, if that's the way things work around here."

He laughed. "It doesn't usually, but I thought I'd better warn you in case that's how things pan out."

"Forewarned. Thank you, sir. Was there anything else?"

"No. Except to wish you all good luck. I'll be keeping a close eye on things during the operation and there for backup should you need me. I wanted to give you my assurance on that."

"Thanks, sir. I'll be out in the field with my team, standing alongside the Inspector of SCO19 for my sins."

"Good luck. Speak to you after the event."

Angie hung up, his words ringing in her ears. *"Speak to you after the event." I wonder if that will be to pull me over the coals or to congratulate me on a job well executed. I hope it's the latter.*

Hours later, after every minute detail had been dissected for what seemed the hundredth time, Angie dismissed her team and requested they report for duty at seven the next morning. She headed home, bone-tired and with the beginning of a headache clawing at her temple.

The house was quiet when she pushed open the front door. "Luke, are you in?" she shouted and soon regretted her actions as the pounding in her head increased.

From somewhere in the house, Luke replied, "Yeah?"

After removing her shoes and hanging her coat in the hallway, she slowly made her way upstairs to the teenager's room. "Can I come in?"

Luke groaned and yanked open the door. "Thanks for disrupting my train of thought, Mum. I really appreciate that."

"Sorry, love. I only wanted to check if you were all right and see what you fancy for dinner. Pardon me for breathing."

"I don't care. Beans on toast or fish fingers and a pile of chips will do me. I need to get this essay finished by tomorrow, and I'm only halfway through the blasted thing."

"Would it be advantageous if you discussed the project with me while I prepare dinner? Like the old days."

"I ain't ancient, Mum. Don't take this the wrong way, but I doubt you'd be able to help with this project."

"What's it about?"

"History."

"And? Yesterday could be regarded as history to some people, love. What particular era in history are we talking about? There might be a glimmer of something I can dredge up in this tiny brain of mine."

"The Hundred Years' War, what do you know about that?" He folded his arms, cocked his head, and waited for her to speak.

She leaned against the doorframe of his room and closed her eyes. *Damn this bloody headache. History used to be my favourite subject at school.* Nuggets of information eased past the building headache. She was determined to show interest in his schoolwork and let him know that he could count on her at least now and again during his assignments. "Okay, here goes; bear in mind that I'm suffering from a headache right now."

"Jeez, that's typical of you and Dad, get the excuses in first before you screw up."

She stood upright, not quite sure whether to be amused or insulted by his comment. She closed her eyes for a few moments before flickering them open and speaking with gusto. "From what I can remember about the subject, the title is grossly misleading as the war actually lasted longer than that. Let me think… it's a little sketchy, but I seem to recall it lasting either one hundred and fifteen years or possibly a little longer." She clicked her fingers and pointed at him. "No, it was a hundred and sixteen years."

He narrowed his eyes. "All right, I'll give you that one. Who was it between?"

"The English and the French, or more to the point, the kings of the relative countries. Here's a fact I bet you don't know."

"Go on, surprise me."

She smiled when the flicker of interest sparked in his eyes, the way it had when she used to bounce him on her knee, filling him with information, which he soaked up like a sponge.

"Did you know that once upon a time, England and France used to be joined?"

"Did they? Or are you messing with me?"

"No, that's what the scientists have deduced over the years. They reckon the sea levels have risen during the centuries and that in around 6500 BC, England broke away from the rest of Europe."

"How fascinating. I'm going to look into that when I get on the Internet this weekend."

"Hey, don't forget we're going away."

He punched the side of his head. "Doh, how could I forget something as exciting as that?"

"Don't you want to go, love? Dad and I thought it would be a great idea to spend some quality time together. We know we've both been guilty of neglecting you over the last few months. This was our way of making it up to you."

"Spending time with the oldies?"

"Thanks! I haven't really thought about myself as being that old. I'm sure your father will be equally as pleased to hear you say that."

"Nah, I'm just teasing. Maybe it would be good to get away, and yes, you're right—you have been neglecting me lately."

Seeing her son crack a smile, even if it was at her expense, was a pleasant change. "Want to help me with the dinner? We could discuss your assignment while we conjure up a fine feast."

Luke surprised her by accepting her second invitation. He stepped out of his room and followed her down to the kitchen. With all the ingredients for the meal pulled from the fridge, Angie gave Luke the chore of peeling the potatoes while she chopped and prepared the other vegetables that would accompany the cottage pie she planned on creating.

The front door slammed, and Warren swept into the kitchen, looking very pleased with himself. "This is unexpected! What's the special occasion?"

"We're discussing the Hundred Years' War. Do you want to add your two pennies' worth?"

Warren held his hands up in front of him. "Umm... think I'll leave that kind of history where it belongs—in the history books. I have enough going on in my mind as it is." He pecked Angie on the cheek and ruffled Luke's already-messy hair. "What's for dinner? I'm starving."

"It comes at a cost," Angie teased.

"Which is?"

"You have to share with us why you're looking so goddamn pleased with yourself."

"Ah, that's a no-brainer. We've only gone and secured yet another huge contract. One of the local solicitor firms wants to hold their monthly staff meetings in our function room starting from the first of next month. If that goes well, they've promised us they'll consider doing all the client wining and dining at the pub in the future."

Angie and Luke high-fived him at the same time.

"That's excellent," Angie said. "I'm proud of you. See what happens when you start to delegate more? How does Haden feel about the extra responsibility involved in something like this?"

"He's well-chuffed. Walked around the pub doing all his tasks this afternoon with a wide grin on his face. Which also means…"

"Yes?"

"That I have no doubts about leaving him to run the pub over the weekend while we're away. We're still going, right? Luke?"

Luke eyed his dad first then glanced at Angie, his expression serious before a smile broke out. "You betcha. Did someone mention going on an adventure break? I fancy beating Dad on the assault course."

"I confess I've only booked us into a holiday cottage down in Cornwall, but we can look the area up later on the net, see if there's an adventure-themed activity park nearby. How's that? I think I'll leave that side of things to you guys, though after what we've got planned tomorrow, I think I'll be in dire need of some good old-fashioned R and R."

Luke returned to peeling the potatoes. "Sounds good to me."

Warren placed an arm around her shoulders and squeezed her tightly. "I can feel your apprehension, love, but I'm sure everything will go according to plan. It usually does."

"Not every time, love. Remember that incident with Lesley? I know she slipped up and got out of position, but I still felt responsible when she took a bullet and had to retire from the force."

"That wasn't your fault, love. She decided to go against your instructions and paid the price. I've told you before that you need to rid yourself of any guilt there."

"I know. It keeps bloody resurfacing when another major operation is about to take place."

"Maybe you need to have a chat with someone about it, if that's the case."

"A psych? Thanks!" Luke chuckled. Angie gave him a clip round the ear. "That's enough from you too."

"It'll help. That's all I'm saying. If the memory continues to haunt you while tackling other ops, then you need to sort it before it starts interfering with your work."

"I'll consider it. To me, going to a shrink is a sign of defeat. Once I go down that route, I wonder if my superiors will end up condemning me for it."

He squeezed her again and planted a sloppy kiss on her forehead. "Your trouble is sometimes you think *too* much."

She dug him in the ribs and continued to prepare the cottage pie.

They enjoyed their meal then, as promised, searched the Internet for an activity centre close to the cottage. They found one a few miles away and rang up to book a day's outing. Satisfied, Luke announced he was going to his room to complete his homework. "Thanks for the input, Mum. I hope I can do it justice now."

"You will, love. I have every faith in you."

Warren and Angie curled up on the sofa and watched a romcom they'd set aside a while ago. The film certainly distracted Angie during the evening, but when it was time for bed, she spent several sleepless hours tossing and turning beside Warren. Eventually, she left the bedroom, collected the spare quilt from the cupboard on the landing, and went downstairs to the lounge. *Great! The night I truly need to get some sleep, and it bloody evades me.*

CHAPTER TWENTY-FIVE

Warren woke Angie with a strong mug of coffee at six in the morning. "Princess, wakey, wakey."

She threw back the quilt, nearly spilling the mug of steaming liquid over herself. "Shit! What time is it?"

"Six. What time did you drift off?"

She wiped the gunk from her eyes and took the mug from his hand. "About four, I think. Crap, I'll down this, have a quick shower and scoot. I wanted to be there at seven this morning."

"Stop panicking. You'll make it in plenty of time. Nervous?"

"The nerves haven't had a chance to kick in yet. They'll be waiting to pounce on me the second I jump behind the steering wheel. You can pretty much guarantee that." She blew on her coffee to cool it down, took a sip then leapt off the sofa. "I better get a move on."

Warren smirked as he watched her tear around the room. "Leave the quilt. I'll tidy up when you leave."

She kissed him firmly on the lips and sprinted up the stairs. She showered, dressed in jeans and a thin jumper then dried her hair before she descended the stairs.

Warren was at the bottom, holding her handbag, a slice of toast and her jacket.

"You're an angel. See you later. I'll touch base with you when I can."

"Stay safe, love. We've got a holiday cottage booked, remember? Love you."

"That's what's keeping me going. Don't worry about me. Be concerned about my team members instead. I hope they've got the experience to pull this thing off."

"They have. Go. Ring me when you can."

Angie struggled into her jacket while trying to eat her breakfast on the move. She was right—once she was settled behind the steering wheel, her nerves began to jangle. Reaching under her seat, she found a plastic bag. She threw the remains of her toast inside and pulled away from the kerb.

The traffic was light that morning. She parked the car in the station car park in record time.

Tommy was waiting to meet her at the front door.

"Everything all right?" she asked.

"Yep, just getting a touch of fresh air before going upstairs. I didn't spot your car, so figured I'd wait for you and escort you into the office."

"You almost sounded genuine for a second there. What's really up?"

"Nothing, just a few jitters. Any tips on how to cope would be appreciated, boss."

Angie tucked her arm through his and steered him through the front door and up the concrete stairs. "Just follow my orders, or when it all kicks off, the orders of

Inspector Davies, the guy leading the SCO19 team. You'll be fine. There's bound to be a few self-doubts flying around until the op gets underway; that's when the adrenaline will kick in. It's a little late for you to back out, if that's what you're really getting at."

He pulled his arm away and stopped mid-flight on the stairs. "I'm not. Crap, I knew if I admitted any doubts, you'd think badly of me."

"Whoa, mister. I'm doing no such thing."

"I'm grand. I just needed to hear a little reassurance. I haven't got anyone at home I can bounce ideas off, boss."

"I know, and I should have thought about that side of things before I questioned your commitment. If it makes you feel any better, I dropped off to sleep at four this morning."

"And you think that's going to make me feel better? Knowing that a zombie is going to be running the show today?" he said light-heartedly.

She laughed and pushed open the office door to a sea of puzzled faces. "Morning, all. Are we ready for this?"

Most of them either nodded or gave her thumbs-up; only Jill seemed a little reluctant. Angie walked towards Jill's desk. "All right, Jill?"

"I will be, once the op is completed, boss."

"I've just had this conversation with Tommy on the way up here. Every single one of us will be battling some form of nerves today. It's not too late if you've decided you don't want to go undercover. No one will think badly of you, I promise."

Jill inhaled and exhaled a few calming breaths. "I'll be okay."

Something about Jill's demeanour caused Angie to doubt the woman's reassuring words. "A trip to the ladies' is needed, I believe. Join me, Jill?"

Without any eye contact, Jill rose from her chair and walked ahead of Angie to the ladies' toilets. Once the door shut behind them, Jill surprised Angie by breaking down in tears.

"Crap, Jill, what's wrong?"

"I'm sorry, boss. I hate to do this to you, especially at this late stage, but I really don't think I can handle this."

"Any specific reason? Because I can assure you, I'm every bit as nervous as you, love."

Jill took a hanky from her sleeve and wiped the tears away. "*Really*? You don't give that impression. You seem so calm."

"I'm not. Although I do think that my experience is keeping the nerves at bay. Look, I'm not going to force anyone into doing anything they don't feel comfortable with. I'm happy to fill your shoes today, if that's really what you want."

Jill's eyes widened. "You *would*? You'd risk your life instead of me?"

"If that's what you think is going on today, yes, in a bloody heartbeat. However, I need to reassure you that we have everything in place with your safety in mind at all times."

"I just can't shift the images of the dead victims up on the wall, boss. I know how ridiculous that sounds, but this side of things is all new to me. I don't want to let you down."

"You won't be. God, I'm glad you confided in me before we placed you in the house." Angie sighed heavily, walked across the room to the full-length mirror on the wall, and studied herself for a moment. *You can do this! You have to do it! We've come too far to back out now! This mission has to take place today, with or without Jill.* She closed her eyes, and when she opened them again, she saw the twinkle of excitement glinting back at her. She turned to face Jill, grabbed the woman's arms, and pulled her into a suffocating embrace. "Wish me luck."

"Good luck, and I can't apologise enough for letting you down."

"Nonsense. Leave me to tell the rest of the team, okay?"

"They're going to frigging hate me." Jill's chin sank onto her chest.

"Don't be silly. They'll appreciate you speaking out, just like I have."

They walked back into the office. Angie clapped to gain everyone's attention as Jill wafted past her in the direction of her desk, her head bowed low to avoid eye contact with her colleagues. "Okay, here's the deal. There's been a change of plan. I'll be taking Jill's place in the operation."

All eyes turned in Jill's direction.

Tommy raised his hand to speak. "It's probably none of my business, but may I ask why?"

"There are a few reasons, but to be honest, we don't have time right now to cover them all. Just know that Jill and I have come to an understanding, and I'm more than happy to swap places with her. You should all recognise what a control freak I am by now. So, Jill, you'll be working alongside Inspector Davies, and I'll be posing as the homeowner while Colin and Frank wait upstairs for the gang to arrive. Any questions?" The team remained silent. "Let's get to the location then. We'll take two cars. I just have to make a quick call first." Angie picked up the telephone and rang DCI Channing. The voicemail kicked in, and Angie sighed. "Hello, sir. This is DI North. I just wanted to inform you that there's been a slight alteration to the plan today. I'll be taking DS Alder's place during the operation. I'll report in when I can. Wish us luck." She hung up, wishing she could have talked directly to her senior officer. *Shit happens!*

The team left the station and arrived close to the house they'd rented specifically for the operation. Angie had called ahead and spoken to Inspector Davies, who'd requested they rendezvous a few streets away to quickly run through the proceedings yet again. He was a little agitated that the details had changed at such a late stage, but he accepted the situation. Angie reassured him the operation would work best having her inside the house to keep a watchful eye on things. Both teams swiftly took up their places, and everyone was ready to get into their roles at nine on the dot. The waiting game had begun.

CHAPTER TWENTY-SIX

Dev and Duke were in one car while the rest of the gang piled into the back of Tyler's newly stolen hatchback. Duke had insisted he wanted to be alone with Dev to ensure everything ran smoothly.

"This is how I want things to go down. We'll let Tyler and Malc take the lead. Once we're inside, I'll be watching the dumb shits like a friggin' hawk. When we've got the stuff that's worth a mint, I'm gonna take their phones off them and find a way of locking those two in the property. We'll dump the stuff in the car and take off. Let the homeowners or cleaners or some other fuckers find them. Those guys need to pay for bringing shit to my door."

"Let's hope it pans out the way you're expecting it to, Duke. Maybe we should come up with a backup plan just in case, eh?"

Duke winked at Dev and tapped the side of his nose. "Already in place, man. Just stick with me, and I'll get us out of here in one piece."

Dev pulled into the road they were looking for. "I hope you're right about this. The ache in my gut tells me something is fishy about this whole deal."

Duke punched his upper arm. "Everything's cool! How did they look to you?"

"Who? Tyler and Malc?"

"Yeah. Who else, man?"

"They seemed pretty chilled. Malc's a shifty guy, but that's probably 'cause he lets his buddy do all the talking and thinking for him. Kinda feel sorry for him, if ya know what I mean."

"Are you serious? What the fuck for? If he was against what Tyler did, he had plenty of chances to speak out—he didn't! So you need to understand that loser is happy to follow the big man's lead—hopefully directly to prison, if we can pull this off today." Duke laughed.

"We'll see. The first sign of trouble, I reckon we get out. Hear me?"

"Hold tight until I can set the fuckers up first. Got that?"

Dev nodded reluctantly and pulled the car to a halt outside the property. The pair climbed out of the car and snapped on their black leather gloves. Tyler, Malc, Billy, Chris, and Todd joined them at the front door to the house.

"Ha, what'cha gonna do? Ring the bell?" Tyler joked, his eyes boring into Duke's.

"Dumb shit, of course I ain't. Let's go round the back and get in through a window where we won't be seen. It's too open out here."

"Think it's wise leaving the cars parked on the drive? What about cameras? Shouldn't we be using clavas or something?" Tyler queried.

"Clavas are for cowards. You wear one if ya want, man. I'm cool like this, 'cause the filth can't lay a finger on me."

"You seem pretty sure about that, Duke," Tyler bit back.

"I am. Less chat, more action. Get your fuckin' arses round the back."

The seven of them rushed to the rear of the property. "The idiots have left the window open. Things are looking good, boys. Chris, climb in and open the back door."

"Wait!" Tyler grabbed Chris's arm. "What if the place is alarmed?"

Todd laughed. "The box is a decoy. I told you, man, this place is a friggin' doddle to get into."

Chris glanced at Todd, and Duke hesitated at the young boy's anxious expression.

"Sweet! What'cha waiting for Chris?"

"What? Want me to go instead?" Todd jumped in.

"Yeah, I've got something wrong with my knee."

Duke laughed. "You're walking all right to me. Step aside then, and let your cuz do your dirty work for ya."

"Give me a leg up." Todd flicked the latch on the top window and slithered his arm inside to unfasten the catch on the main window below. He entered the kitchen and unlocked the back door to let the rest of the gang in.

The men walked through the kitchen and into the hallway. The house was silent.

"So, Todd, you're the expert on this place. We'll follow your lead," Duke announced loudly.

Todd nodded. "Okay, all the best art is in the lounge. In here." He pushed open the double wooden-panelled doors and stopped dead.

Sitting in the winged armchair, next to a roaring fire, was a woman.

"Shit!" Duke shouted. "Who the fuck are you?"

"I could say the same thing. How dare you come into my home uninvited! Get out before I call the police."

Duke rushed past Todd and grabbed the woman before she had the chance to reach for the phone lying on the table beside her. He yanked the phone wire out of the wall and tussled with the woman as he tried to tie her wrists together.

"What the hell are you lot staring at? Help me. Chris, take over here. Make sure her wrists are tied nice and tight. You'll stop struggling if you know what's good for you, bitch," Duke sneered, inches from the woman's face. He watched the terrified expression as she scanned the room. "You should be scared. Keep quiet, and you might get out of this alive."

Todd approached the woman. "You were supposed to be on holiday, dumb bitch."

The woman narrowed her eyes and glared at him. "I trusted you and your mother. If this is how you repay that trust… you better get far away from London once you're finished here. I'll get you and your bloody mother for this. Don't think you'll get away with it."

Todd pushed the woman back into her chair, and she winced when she leaned back against her tied hands.

"Enough of this shit. I say we grab the gear and get outta here, quick smart!" Tyler suggested urgently, his gaze taking in the artwork decorating the walls. "Where's the safe, whore?"

The woman's mouth clamped shut. She looked Tyler up and down as though he were a piece of shit. "You think I'm going to tell you that?"

Tyler slapped the woman hard around the face. Todd jumped in to prevent him from striking her again. "Pack it in, man. She can't tell us if you knock her out cold, can she? Anyway, I know it's upstairs in the bedroom."

"Show me," Tyler demanded, snatching his arm from Todd's grasp.

"Now, now, children, play nicely," Duke teased, amused by the men's shenanigans.

Tyler shook his head. "Glad you think it's fuckin' funny. I think we should grab the stuff and get out of here quick; I don't trust her. She's too cool. You got some kind of secret buzzer around here that goes direct to the cop shop, or what?"

"No. Untie me. I'm insured. Take what you want. I can show you where the safe is."

Tyler snarled. "Nice try, lady. *We're* in charge, not *you*. Sit there and keep your trap shut."

"Leave her alone. Come, I'll show you where it is." Todd darted out of the room, and Tyler and Malc followed him.

Duke paced the floor for a few minutes, to let the woman stew. He walked over to the window just as a thud upstairs made him look up at the ceiling. Shouts broke out. "What the fuck are they playing at up there? Chris, Billy, go find out." The boys left the room, and Duke's eye was drawn to a bush in the garden. "Here, Dev."

Dev stood beside him and Duke pointed at the bush. "Shit man, it's a fuckin' trap. I bet that's fuckin' armed police."

The shouting upstairs increased. Duke's mind raced at a hundred miles an hour, searching for the answers to get him out of this mess. One scenario prodded his temple. He pushed Dev out of the way when he heard the others charging down the stairs. Duke yanked the woman out of the chair and placed her in front of him.

Duke's pals barged into the room with two strangers. "What the fuck is going on here?" he demanded. "Who the fuck are these two?"

He was confused. His temper raged as he watched Todd push Tyler and Malc ahead of him. Chris and Billy were restrained by the men who had joined them upstairs.

"The game's up, Duke," Todd finally spoke.

"You double-crossing piece of shit, you're a pig! I should've bloody known. I ain't going down without a fight, man."

Todd shook his head. "Then you'll be the loser, Duke. This place is surrounded by armed police."

"Like I give a shit. I'm getting out of here with her." His eyes narrowed when he watched the anxiety mount in Todd's eyes. "Wait a fuckin' minute! She's one of you lot, ain't she?"

Todd raised his hand. "There's no need for anyone to get hurt. Look, here's the deal, man: we're after the murderers," he said, thumbing towards Tyler and Malc. "I know what they did, and I know you didn't order or agree with it. Let's get them behind bars where they belong and stop all this other shit, yeah?"

"Fuck off! You think I'm stupid? You'll dump tons of other charges on me the second you slap on the cuffs. I ain't having none of that. I'll take my chances and get out of here, and *she's* coming with me."

"Leave it! Just arrest Tyler and Malc and let Duke leave the house."

"But, boss, I can't let that happen."

"Boss! You let a *bitch* boss you around! Are you kidding?"

Todd exhaled a deep breath.

Duke laughed. "Something tells me you shouldn't have blurted that out, man. She's gonna snip your balls off when, I mean *if*, she meets up with you again."

"I won't," the woman reassured Todd.

Duke placed his forearm around her throat and pulled her viciously against him. "I ain't letting go of this filthy pig. She's my ticket out of here."

"I promise not to struggle."

"Damn right, you won't." He withdrew a flick knife from his back pocket and touched the blade against her cheek, nicking it with a tiny cut to emphasise his point.

"Hey, Duke, there's no need to hurt her," Dev urged. He raced over to the window.

"Any movement out there?"

Dev strained his neck a little more. "I can't see anything. Wait! I can make out two guys in black."

Duke jerked the arm he was holding around the woman's neck. "How many are out there?"

"I don't have a clue," the woman replied.

He placed the blade against her throat. "It makes no odds to me if I kill ya, lady. How many?" His gaze held Todd's, warning him what would happen if he attempted any kind of rescue.

The woman gulped noisily, and he felt the lump go down her throat. "At least twenty."

Duke pulled the woman backwards to join Dev at the window.

She stumbled a little and clung to his forearm, trying to loosen his grip on her throat.

"Jesus, man, we ain't gonna get outta here alive with that mob outside."

Dev shook his head. "Take the woman and go, before they've got a chance to call for even more backup, Duke."

"What's the plan, bitch? To force us out or are they gonna storm the place?"

"They're hoping you'll hand yourselves in peacefully."

"Some hope of that happening. Okay, let me think about this."

Dev pushed him. "Duke, there's no time to think. Get outta here now. Don't worry about me. Just take her and go, man."

"Why ain't you gonna come with me?"

"I ain't up for this. I'll sit it out here, take what's coming to me. Take your chance and fly!"

"I ain't leaving you. You're my bro. Get ready; we'll go out the back way."

"And do what?"

"Whatcha saying?"

"I'm saying I think you should go out the front way. She's important. They ain't gonna risk shooting her."

"You're being foolish," Todd shouted from behind. "You step one foot out of here, and the trained marksmen will put you down in seconds. Give yourselves up. I've told you it's Tyler and Malc we're really after, not you."

Duke jerked his forearm again. "You think that's the way this should go down, lady?"

"Scott is talking sense. We can't pin anything on either you or Dev. You'll walk away from here a free man if you let us go. Of course, that'll change if you do what you're suggesting. These guys don't fool around if one of their own is in danger."

Tyler laughed. "She's playing ya, man. They both are. You're as much in the shit as we are. You won't get out of here alive. Every gun out there will be trained on ya, ready to riddle your body with bullets the second you try and escape."

He exhaled loudly, unsure what to do, for once in his life. *Where's Leroy when I need him most?*

Dev snuck up behind him and whispered in his ear, "Stop stalling and don't listen to that prick. He knows fuck all."

"I'm going—we're going." Duke walked towards the door.

Angie dug in her heels, making it difficult for Duke to control her. He nicked the side of her cheek again and felt drops of her blood hit his forearm.

"Don't be a hero, sweetheart." He was wary as he passed by the three coppers. Todd tried to prevent him from leaving. He received a busted nose for his efforts. "Fuck off, Todd, or whateva your blasted name is."

"Scott! Let him take me and that's heroine not hero."

"Whateva! You tell 'em, or I'll shaft ya as soon as we get outta here."

"What's to say you won't do that anyway?" the woman asked in a strained voice.

Duke laughed. "I'll keep ya on yer toes, lady."

Shouting came from the room they'd just left as one of the coppers told the men outside what was going on.

"It's not too late. You don't have to do this, Duke."

"Shut up! Let me think," Duke hissed. He pulled open the front door and shoved the woman out first.

"Hold your fire, men! Don't shoot!" A man dressed in black with a bulletproof vest stepped out from behind a nearby bush. "Let the woman go."

"Not going to happen. I'm getting outta here, and she's my ticket. Back off, man!"

"I can't allow that. Leave the police officer here."

"You think I'm dumb? I leave her behind and I'll be dead within minutes."

"Okay, if that's the way you want to play it. Men, take up your weapons, take aim, and…"

"Inspector, don't do this! I won't allow you to put my boss's life in jeopardy." A woman popped up from behind another bush and pulled on the officer's arm.

He threw her off him. "I'm in charge around here, not you."

The woman in Duke's grasp shouted, "I'll be fine. Let him go, please. The murderers you're after are inside with my officers; this man hasn't done anything wrong."

"And what happens when you leave the area with this man? Have you thought about that, DI North?" the officer snapped.

"I'll be fine. He's assured me that he'll let me go as soon as we've left the area."

"Nice one, lady," Duke mumbled in the woman's ear.

"This is my butt on the line, North, not yours. Are you going to admit this was your idea at a disciplinary hearing?"

"Yes, if necessary. Stand down, Inspector, please."

The Inspector's gaze bore into Duke's. He obviously wasn't keen on taking orders from a woman. He threw his arms up in the air. "Go, you're free to go! This is on your head, North."

"I understand. Don't let the others out of your sight; they're the ones we need to arrest."

"Tyler and Malc are the ones. Dev, Chris and Billy have done nothing, ya hear me?" Duke shouted.

"Jill, ensure that happens, okay?"

"Yes, boss."

"Enough chitchat—we're getting in the car now," Duke informed the onlookers. He steered the woman towards the vehicle he and Dev had arrived in. After shoving her in the driver's side in front of him, he forced her over into the next seat. Holding the tip of the knife under her chin, Duke started up the engine. Dozens of armed police appeared on all sides of the driveway, but no one tried to prevent them from leaving. "Ya done good, lady. Ya might just have kept yourself alive."

"Good, I'm planning on spending the weekend with my husband and my son."

Duke laughed. "You cocky bitch, I ain't doing you no favours; just 'cause you ain't dressed like a pig... the second we leave this area, I'm gonna dump ya, after I slit your throat."

CHAPTER TWENTY-SEVEN

Angie's mind matched the speed of her racing heart. He put his foot down and sped away on the gravel drive. The angry looks of the armed officers they left behind did nothing to ease the dread of what was about to happen to her. *I've cocked-up. I should never have willingly left with him. Now I'm the prisoner with no way out of this.* His vile threat lingered in her ears as they left the area. She searched her mind, back to her training days all those years ago, to the lessons regarding hostage taking. It didn't help—all the advice she sought disappeared into thin air when she needed it the most. She closed her eyes, hoping for divine inspiration, but none came.

Duke put his foot down harder, one hand holding the knife under her chin, the other gripping the wheel firmly. His gaze darted around the windscreen, the rear-view, and his wing mirrors. Angie had to do something; she could sense his anxiety rising with every passing moment. The blade nicked her chin when she swallowed. She held her breath. *Do it! I have to do it before time runs out!*

She jiggled her hands and the cord Chris had loosely tied around her wrists slipped off. Clenching her right hand into the tightest ball she could manage, she screamed like a woman possessed as she lashed out at him. The car swerved, and the knife escaped his grasp, ending up at her feet.

"You bitch! Ya think ya can get out of this? You're wrong, woman."

"We'll see about that."

Angie reached down and searched under the edge of her seat for the knife. Her fingertips grazed the handle, but she couldn't grasp it with her hand. Duke battled to keep the car under control as he suddenly landed a right hook, hitting her in the mouth. Dazed, she fell back against the headrest. His arm swept past her, and he pulled on the door handle. Before she had a chance to launch another attack, his arm threw open the passenger door. She watched the ground speeding past and regretted her lack of concentration when she felt him shove her out of the car. Angie screamed as her body was jettisoned from the speeding vehicle.

She rolled across the tarmac like a keg of beer. Duke's car remained in her sight until it turned into the adjoining road. Finally, when her body came to a grinding halt, her head hit the kerb with a deafening thump. Behind her, in the distance, car tyres screeched on the road. Over the noise of the running engine, she could hear angry voices shouting, then heavy footsteps laboured to a standstill close to her head.

"Is she all right? Ring for an ambulance, Frank."

Angie tried to reply, to assure them that she was okay, but the urgency of her unheard internal voice was extinguished by swiftly descending darkness.

Someone was squeezing her hand and gently stroking her cheek.

"Is that you, God?" Angie uttered, her mouth as dry as blotting paper.

"Bloody hell, you've called me some names over the years, but never that."

The sound of her husband's voice made her feel safe. She felt his lips brush hers before he sat down on the bed beside her. Angie's eyes opened slowly. Her vision was blurred, and she blinked them shut again. "What the hell hit me? A bloody lorry?"

Warren chuckled. "I better let DCI Channing fill you in."

"Shit, is he here?" She attempted to sit up.

Warren clamped his hands on her shoulders. "Oh no, you don't. The doctor said you need to rest, lady. Yes, he's here. He seems a decent chap to me, and yes, I've covered you up before you ask."

Angie smiled and tried to open her eyes again. This time her vision was a little clearer. She surveyed the room to see who else was there with them. "Hello, sir, come to give me a bollocking in person, have you?"

"Not exactly, DI North, although the thought had crossed my mind the instant I was told about your *accident*."

"I'm sorry, sir. But the suspect left me with little choice. I had to go with him."

"Understandable. We'll let this one slide, eh? How are you feeling?" His smile seemed genuine enough.

She coughed slightly. "I'd be lying if I told you I felt on top of the world."

"I'm not surprised. Anyway, I just thought I'd drop by and bring you up to speed on a few things. Thought it might aid your recuperation knowing that the suspects are all behind bars."

"All of them? Including Duke Mason, sir?"

"Sadly no. In spite of all our desperate efforts to capture the gang leader, he managed to escape our grasp."

Her heart sank. "That's a shame. Has he gone underground? What about the other gang members? Can you offer them some kind of deal in the hope they'll tell you where he is?"

"We've tried every trick available to us. No luck, I'm afraid. Maybe there is honour amongst thieves after all. Okay, I'm out of here. You're under strict orders to take next week off and only to return to work when you're fully recovered. Is that understood, Inspector?"

She smiled at his generosity. "Understood, sir, thank you."

"No, it should be me and the team thanking you, Inspector, for putting your life in danger the way you did. I'm extremely fortunate to have such a class act running our team."

Angie's cheeks warmed. "Thank you, sir. Before you leave, promise me you'll look into the arrest made by Meadows and release that innocent man. Damn! I've forgotten his name."

"I was just on my way to do that now. Rest, Inspector, that's an order."

DCI Channing shook hands with Angie and Warren, then left the room.

"Nice guy. Unlike the last monster you worked under," Warren said, leaning in for another kiss. "I've missed you."

"Given the circumstances, forgive me if I don't return that statement. I have no idea what I'm feeling right now. I forgot to ask if he thinks the charges will stick against the gang members."

"Trust you to always think about work. Yes, I asked him that myself. He seemed pretty confident that the murder charges and assaults would stick, not sure about Dev's and Chris's involvement. Did I get their names right?"

"You did. Yeah, I'd agree with that. We've done a deal with Chris anyway, but from the looks of things, Dev wasn't in control any more than the others. He was probably more the brains of the outfit, although I suppose he was guilty of coming up with that scam in the first place. We'll have to wait and see. I'm disappointed they haven't tracked down Duke yet. They could fling attempted murder at him if they ever catch up with the bastard. I'd happily have my day in court with that charge over his head."

"Hey, less talk about work issues. You're supposed to be recovering. I had a word with the doctor, and he assured me that, providing you gained consciousness and the tests were positive, we could still go away for the weekend. Of course, that's entirely up to you."

"Damn right I'm still going. Perhaps we can extend it for a few extra days? I'm under orders to take next week off, remember?"

Warren rubbed his chin as he thought. "Perhaps I could leave the pub in Haden's capable hands until Wednesday. How's that?"

Her spirits rose. "That would be wonderful. Do you think Luke will be okay with that too?"

"I don't see why not. He sends his love. He was a little disappointed that I ordered him to go to school. He wanted to be here when you woke up."

"That's good to hear. He's a good kid. Let's hope this holiday gives us what we're seeking and more. For all our sakes."

Angie was dismissed from hospital the next day. Luke and Warren collected her and swept her away to the holiday cottage in Cornwall. They spent fun-filled, relaxing days in the cottage's pretty garden and at the beach. The day that Warren whisked an excited Luke off to the activity centre gave Angie the time and solitude to reflect on how lucky she was to have escaped her ordeal. She'd learned that in a moment's notice, plans could change, and those changes could have a drastic effect. People often forgot what was important to them until it was too late. She vowed that from that day forward, her family would always come first.

EPILOGUE

Duke clenched his fists. His eyes bore into the face of the policewoman who had shattered his plans. DI North of Scotland Yard had survived unharmed. The television had replayed the story for the last few days, and Duke couldn't help but watch. The arrests. Their victory. *His* wanted face.

He muted the noise; the sound of his name linked to the murder cases enraged him. He threw the remote control at the screen and pounded the coffee table. *How the fuck could I have let this happen?* Regret washed over him as he reflected on the decisions he'd made in the last month.

"Breaking my TV ain't gonna help ya, lad."

Duke watched Alan stroll round the sofa. "I know, man. I'm sorry."

He stood up and paced the shoebox living room of a terrace house in Harlesden. Not his own home filled with his possessions. Not his postcode. Not even his clothes. Anger coursed through Duke's veins as he thought of everything he'd lost.

After dumping the car near Lambeth Station, Duke had known it was impossible for him to return home. Any location or person associated with him was sure to be swarming with cops. He'd jumped on an underground train and ventured into northwest London, to the only person he knew would hide him—Alan 'All Jobs' Becker. Alan, fifteen years Duke's senior, had been Leroy's mentor and still had power and influence in the gang network.

"Duke, you need to chill out and stop worrying." Alan laughed and lit his spliff.

"I'm on the fucking run!"

"So you hide out here. They'll soon forget about 'ya."

Duke sank back into the armchair and held his head in his hands. "And then what?"

When no response came, Duke was forced to look up. Alan's eyes were fixed on him; a serious expression fell over the man's dark features.

"Then you start again, my dear boy," Alan finally said. "Learn from these mistakes, Duke, because they'll be the making of you. Run away now, and you'll be running forever, always looking over your shoulder. Take some time and prepare yourself. Stand up for yourself, and it will shape who you are and the power you can have. If that's still what you want?"

"Of course," Duke fired back without hesitation.

Alan smirked. "Then it ain't over. You just need to decide your next move."

The man took a long pull on his joint, exhaled slowly, and eased back into his seat. Duke couldn't take his eyes off Alan, grateful for his help and guidance but also in awe of his wisdom. Alan had pushed him in the right direction, and Duke knew what he had to do. No longer would he pity himself. No longer would he trust anyone.

The images of Tyler, Malc and the coppers who had hoodwinked him flooded his mind. He was consumed with hate. He had to be patient, lay low, and even become invisible for quite a while. But that wouldn't be impossible, not with Alan on his side.

Duke accepted the large rolled-up joint. "I'll get my revenge. One way or another I'll get my revenge on them all."

The End

Thank you for reading The Caller; we sincerely hope you enjoyed reading this novel as much as we loved writing it.

If you liked it, please consider posting a short review as genuine feedback is what makes all the lonely hours writers spend producing their work worthwhile.

Sign up to our newsletters via our Facebook pages to hear about our new releases as they happen.

Made in the USA
Charleston, SC
06 June 2016